PRAISE FOR
ROBERT MAGARIAN

Praise for *The Watchman*

"*The Watchman* came to life for me, because it is so well written and instills a sense of caution as you read. I am delighted to have had the pleasure of discovering Robert Magarian and his talent."
—Bea Kunz, Amazon reviewer

Praise for *72 Hours*

"I was compelled to carry *72 Hours* around with me. It's a blend of trouble both personal and political, with an evil that will stop at nothing and a CDC that may—or may not—have found the only salvation. Here, also, is a family in pain. Suspenseful, timely, and breath-catching."
—Carolyn Wall, author of *Sweeping Up Glass*

Praise for *You'll Never See Me Again*

"I absolutely loved this book, I couldn't put it down. The details and thought put into this book by Dr. Magarian are absolutely amazing. I felt as if I was in the book myself."
—Brooke, Amazon reviewer

"Loved the book. It kept my attention, kept me guessing and kept me reading. I didn't want to put it down. Highly recommend it."
—Nancy Loyd, Amazon reviewer

Praise for *Follow Your Dream*

"In *Follow Your Dream*, Robert Magarian provides a template for turning a dream into reality, step-by-step. In 1987 Magarian created the first annual Norman Community Christmas Dinner, serving a free meal to individuals and family who would have been alone on Christmas Day. In the years hence, the event has grown to serve 1,600 people, with 200 volunteers. This is a remarkable story of what one person can do with a dream and how that dream can change many lives."
—Robert L. Ferrier, Amazon reviewer

ALSO BY ROBERT MAGARIAN

Fiction

72 Hours

You'll Never See Me Again: A Crime to Remember

Essays

Follow Your Dream

A Journey into Faith

THE
WATCHMAN

A NOVEL

BY

ROBERT MAGARIAN

Copyright © 2007, 2016 by Robert Magarian

All rights reserved.

ISBN (print): 0-9973348-2-7
ISBN-13 (print): 978-0-9973348-2-1
ISBN (ebook): 0-9973348-4-3
ISBN-13 (ebook): 978-0-9973348-4-5

Publisher's Note: This is a work of fiction. Names, characters, places, and incidents either are the product of the author's imagination or are used fictitiously. Any resemblance to persons, living or dead is entirely coincidental.

Author Photo: "shevyvision"
shevaun williams & associates, Norman, OK
www.shevaunwilliams.com

Editing: Nancy Hancock

Print Formatting: By Your Side Self-Publishing
www.ByYourSideSelfPub.com

DEDICATION

This book is dedicated to the loving memory of Leon K. Magarian and Mary Beth Stanaszek. They left us much too early.

"…and the people of the land take a man from them, and make him their Watchman."

Ezekiel 33:2

CHAPTER ONE

The Secretary of Defense wanted his antibiological.

Matt Brenner arrived in his lab around eight o'clock on June 24, 1997, and sat at his computer, striking keys at a rapid pace to finish his research report. The work with Fabor Keyes at Stanford had progressed beyond his expectations, and now his time there was about to end.

His lifelong ambition to work with his childhood friend, Jack Sinclair, was about to happen. As he stood and squared the papers, the intercom buzzed. He pressed the switch. Mildred, the departmental secretary, announced that he had a phone call.

He lifted the phone.

"Matt Brenner," he said, sitting down.

"Matt, this is Jack."

"Where are you?"

"St. Louis Union Station. I slipped in here to call you."

A tinge of fear struck Matt. "What's wrong, Jack?"

"Don't have much time. I'm being followed. Just listen."

Sensing fear in his friend's voice, Matt obeyed.

"A terrible thing has happened. Six homeless men have died God-awful deaths in abandoned buildings here. I believe they could have been used in an experiment."

The book *Extreme Measures* flashed into Matt's mind.

"A week before the homeless men were found, three of my Russian neurotoxins came up missing," said Jack. "We were trying to develop antidotes for them. That's what's got me puzzled. Don't know why the military used them on the homeless guys. We already knew the horrible effects of the neurotoxins."

"Why is the military following you?"

1

"I have something they want."
"What do you have?"
"It's—Oh, shit. I gotta go."
"Jack, wait!"
A click and then nothing.

CHAPTER TWO

Matt bolted upright in bed, his heart pounding. He rubbed his head and looked at the clock on the nightstand. Four a.m. He lay back and stared up at the ceiling. "Jack, I hope you're okay." He had tried all last evening to contact Jack at his lab, and at his home. No answers.

Sitting at the kitchen table, drinking coffee from a large Stanford University cup, Matt stared into space, thinking about a way to help Jack, but he couldn't concentrate.

He rose and went into the living room of his one-bedroom apartment, stopped at his desk, reached for the phone, and pressed in the numbers for DnaTech Pharmaceuticals. He asked the switchboard operator for Jack Sinclair's lab. After seven rings, he hung up, grabbed his briefcase, and darted out the door. He drove to the molecular biology building on the Stanford campus, parked in the first open slot, and entered through the backdoor. He took the steps two at a time to the second floor. He avoided elevators. Besides running in the mornings, he liked to race up and down the steps twice a day for ten minutes for cardiovascular health. He arrived in the lab around eight-thirty, moved to his desk against the wall, swapped his light sport coat for a white jacket, and sat with his back to his desk, glancing around the room.

The beige walls reflected just the right amount of illumination from the fluorescent ceiling lights in two rooms about ninety by thirty feet. Each lab had the latest technology in research equipment dispersed throughout.

"Those DNA results are ready, Matt," said Harriet French, his research associate, moving to the front from her workbench. A technician, seated at the biohazard hood up front, pipetted samples of bacterial DNA into rows of glass vials.

He nodded. "I'll check them later."

Harriet, a thirty-three-year-old brunette with an athletic body that women would die for, turned eyes when she moved through the halls. She not only had a great body, but also a great mind, and a doctorate in genetics from Columbia.

Matt had placed his desk and computer against the front wall, so his back would be to the workers to frustrate interruptions. The slamming of cabinet doors and metal stools scraping across the floor didn't bother him, but interruptions got to him. He turned to his desk, lifted the phone, dialed DnaTech, and asked the operator to put him through to Dr. Sinclair's lab.

This time he got someone.

"Silvia."

"Jack Sinclair. This is Matt Brenner." He rubbed a hand over the report in front of him.

"I'm... I'm sorry, sir, but I'm not supposed to talk about it to anyone."

His pulse quickened. "About what? Is it about Jack? We're friends."

He heard her inhale and exhale. "Dr. Sinclair... he... he died last night in his Level 3. It was an accident."

Matt jumped up, hitting his leg against the metal desk; the crash resonated throughout the lab. Startled lab workers glanced up at him. He felt dizzy, and he braced himself against the desk. The lab became quiet, and he could hear his heart hammering. Sitting down, he picked up the phone and asked Silvia how it happened. While he waited for her response, images of Jack's body ravaged by some agent flashed in his mind.

"One of the Russian neurotoxins got loose on him."

"Who found him?"

"Dr. Peter Crane. Around eleven o'clock."

"Can you transfer me to Dr. Crane?"

"I'm sorry. I can't." The phone went dead.

Matt took a deep breath and stared at the wall. He wondered if anyone had notified Jack's sister, Sandra. He reached for his directory, lifted the phone, and dialed her number.

"Sandra? This is Matt. I just heard about Jack. I'm shocked."

She sniffled, then sighed. "Poor Jack. Just got word a few hours ago."

"Sandra. I want to help."

"Hadn't heard from Jack in several months, and this morning Colonel Jagger called me. He said Jack's death was an accident, but a thorough investigation was underway." She paused. "Can we trust him?"

"Don't know. Let me do some checking. I'll be in touch. Okay?"

"Okay," she said in a whisper.

Matt broke the circuit and dialed DnaTech's number. This time he asked for Peter Crane, but the operator told him Dr. Crane wouldn't return for a week. He slammed down the phone. He had never felt this helpless. He swallowed hard. He didn't think he could trust the military, not after reading the *Newsweek* article, but he would never tell Sandra. The article had exposed the Department of Defense for testing chemicals and biologicals on US soldiers without their knowledge.

Matt thought about going to the civilian authorities, but he had no proof that Jack was killed. Anyway, he had a feeling they wouldn't go after the military. Everyone knew the military had their own justice. But what if he got hard evidence? Maybe the FBI would do something. Harriet's voice brought him out of his thoughts.

"What's wrong, Matt?" He saw compassion in her eyes.

"My best friend is dead," he said.

"Was he ill?"

"The military said it was a lab accident, but I think he was murdered."

"Murdered?" she said with raised brows.

Matt nodded. "He called me, scared out of his wits. I think someone was after him." He paused to regain his composure. "Give me a few minutes, will you?"

She moved to the lab bench near Matt's desk and peered into a microscope. A short time later, Matt ran fingers through his blond hair, stood, and approached Harriet.

"Your significant other—he's a detective, right?"

She looked puzzled. "So you really believe your friend was murdered?"

"Yes. I'd like to meet with him at his office. Can you arrange it?"

"Certainly."

"Thanks. I have to see Keyes." He grabbed his report and rushed into the corridor.

Fluorescent lights gleamed off pristine walls, making the corridor appear large. Matt passed researchers in white lab coats, and dodged two technicians who shot out of labs, carrying trays of steaming glassware.

He stepped into Mildred's office. She was a thin, fifty-five-year-old with gray-streaked black hair. Her gold-rimmed glasses covered half her face. She looked up and smiled.

"He's in."

Dr. Fabor Keyes kept his door ajar, making himself available at anytime to the members of his research team. Matt pushed the door open, tapped on the doorjamb, and waited.

Keyes, a Nobel Laureate in genetics, won his prize for work demonstrating that bacteria transferred genes from one to another in a manner akin to sexual intercourse. An intense man in his fifties, and then some, he was the director of the molecular biology department. He also was a consultant to the scientists at Fort Detrick, Maryland, at the Army Medical Research Institute of Infectious Diseases (USAMRIID). Matt had come from the Institute almost two years earlier.

Keyes stood under five-foot-five, with narrow hips and small hands, liked to dress casual—open shirt collars and sweaters without sleeves. Matt only saw him in suits at scientific meetings. Keyes looked up from his writing when he heard the knock. Matt thought, with his pointed nose and thin mustache, he favored William Faulkner.

"Sit anywhere," he said, waving a hand. "Move that stack of folders to the floor."

Matt stepped over papers, but didn't sit.

The office seemed small. Keyes despised filing, but wouldn't allow anyone to touch anything. Floor-to-ceiling bookshelves covered the wall behind his desk. Books with strips of yellow legal pad paper slipped between pages, leaned to one side. Stacks of scientific reprints filled several shelves. Other stacks occupied part of the floor, his desk, and the tops of two filing cabinets. His ability to retrieve specific articles from these stacks amazed his researchers.

To calm himself, Matt glanced at several pictures on the wall next to the window. Keyes had been Scientific Advisor to the President and appeared in several pictures with him and the Vice President.

Matt moved to the chairman's desk and placed his report on it, a report on chimerical mice, genetically altered to have a human immune system.

Keyes glanced at it, then looked up. "Something wrong?"

"My friend, Jack Sinclair, is dead." Matt moved to the chair and flopped into it. "They found him in his lab last night."

Keyes took his time answering. "I'm really sorry, Matt. I know you two were very close."

"His lab tech told me one of his toxins got loose on him. I don't believe it. Jack was always very careful."

"You must take some time off."

He looked into Keyes' brown eyes and shook his head. Matt told him about Jack's phone call and about the experiments performed on six homeless men in St. Louis.

"So you think someone in the military used the homeless as guinea pigs?"

"I don't really know. Jack thought they did." He paused. "I only know that someone at DnaTech killed Jack."

"That'll be hard to prove," said Keyes.

"I promised Jack's sister I'd do something."

Keyes frowned. "Don't get involved in this. Let the military handle it."

Matt rose and stopped at the door. "Maybe Peter Crane can help."

"I'll give David Rutherford a call," said Keyes.

Back at his desk, Matt thought about Jack. They had grown up together on farms in Iowa, and after graduating from high school, Matt went to Chicago and Jack to Harvard for their undergraduate degrees in chemistry and genetics. Matt convinced Jack to come to the University of Chicago for graduate study in molecular biology. Neither he nor Jack liked the idea of working for the Army, but their advisor at Chicago convinced them to give it a try. Matt went to USAMRIID and Jack to the Biodefense Center in DnaTech Pharmaceuticals.

Harriet's voice brought him out of his thoughts. "Here's William's number. He'll see you whenever you like."

————◆————

Matt opened the tall glass door leading into the lobby of the Palo Alto Police station. The only person he saw was a female officer sitting at a desk behind a glass enclosure. He walked across the room to the window and asked for Detective William Purvis, speaking through a circular opening in the window. She nodded and picked up a phone. Moments later, the door next to her station opened and out stepped a six-foot medium-built man with a narrow face, holding a Styrofoam cup in his hand.

"I'm looking for Detective William Purvis," said Matt.

"You've found him. You must be Dr. Brenner."

"I am."

He waved Matt in. As the door closed behind them, Matt followed Purvis, taking it all in. The room was spacious with a large open area in the middle and cubicles along the walls. Men and women in uniforms, and some in street clothes, sat at their desks focused on paperwork or on their computer screens. As Purvis led him to the corner cubicle, Matt saw a young man in handcuffs, sitting at a table between two standing detectives in a conference room.

Purvis set the coffee cup on his desk, unbuttoned his suit coat, and sat.

Matt slipped into the only chair next to the desk.

"Harriet tells me you have a problem with the military."

"It's about a friend of mine who worked for the Army in St. Louis.

I believe someone killed him."

He frowned. "Guess you don't have any proof of that," he said, reaching for his cup.

"Not at the moment. But if I get some, what next?"

"You're not planning on taking them on by yourself, are you?"

"There's no one else."

The detective shook his head. "I wouldn't recommend it."

He paused, taking a sip of coffee.

"Dr. Brenner. I don't want to insult your intelligence, but maybe you've got it all wrong. You could be overreacting."

"Dammit! I'm not overreacting."

Matt locked on his gaze.

"Listen, Detective. My friend called me scared to death. Someone was following him, and now he's dead."

"William. Call me William."

"Okay, William." Matt, sitting erect in his chair, explained that Jack knew the Army had used the neurotoxins from his lab on the homeless men, and that he had something the military was after.

"I see. Guess you don't know what it was he had in his possession?"

Matt shook his head. "Don't know. Can you help me or not?"

"First, you'll have to get proof that someone actually killed him. When you get that, you can test the homicide division in the St. Louis PD. But let me warn you. They won't be willing to take on the military."

"And if they don't?"

He finished off his coffee and rose. "If that doesn't work, go to the FBI. Here's my card."

Matt stood and reached for it.

"Call me at that number, if you need the name of a person in the St. Louis Field Office. That's the best I can do for you."

CHAPTER THREE

Major General Princeton Taylor, the Pentagon's antiterrorism guru, squirmed into a comfortable position in a leather chair at his neat desk. He took a sip of coffee and reached for the Monday morning intelligence briefing. His temper flared when he read about terrorist cells in the Middle East, and then subsided when his thoughts turned to his plan to rid the world of them. He didn't subscribe to the Joint Chief's wait-and-see philosophy. They were busy playing politics, putting the country in grave danger. Soon his biological would be ready, and no one could stop him.

The intercom buzzed. Taylor pressed the lever without looking up. "Yes."

"Sir, General Whitehead's office is on one."

He pressed the button. "This is General Taylor."

The female voice on the other end said that General Whitehead would like to see him in his office in the next few minutes. Arriving on the third floor in the E-ring, Taylor followed Whitehead's secretary into the three-star general's office, next to the offices of the Secretary of Defense. Speaking on the phone, Whitehead gestured for him to sit. Taylor settled into one of the two leather side-arm chairs. Cigar smoke irritated Taylor's nose.

Whitehead hung up the phone.

"Princeton, that was the boss," he said, referring to the Secretary of Defense, Lewis Corwin. "He's pleased with the way you built the Biodefense Center."

Taylor smiled, feeling pleased with himself. Two years earlier, the DoD had changed its strategy against terrorism, which led to this secret facility in St. Louis. The Pentagon had decided in the mid-

1990s to broaden its biodefense research program and to build a site to produce vaccines, since pharmaceutical companies saw no profit in producing them. A design for the Army's proposed facility had been completed, but no site selected. Several members of Congress ordered the Army to stop until it completed a study to justify the need for such a facility. They believed the military had no reason to get into the drug business.

Obsessed with the vastness of the Russians' arsenal of biologicals, and the Middle East terrorists, the Department of Defense couldn't wait. Their concept of war had changed. New antidotes and vaccines were needed. The DoD secretly looked for a hidden site. That search led to a biotech company in the Midwest known as DnaTech Pharmaceutical, Inc., nestled at the edge of Clayton, Missouri, a suburb of St. Louis. Dr. David Rutherford III was its President and CEO.

Rutherford's biotech company faced bankruptcy, and he needed money to save it. He and Defense Secretary Corwin struck a deal. The DoD leased the top two floors and installed a mammoth security system in and around the building. The DoD would pay a handsome yearly sum, and DnaTech would produce the vaccines and antidotes.

Taylor installed the latest equipment for biodefense research on the top floor, calling it the Center for Biodefense Research. On the fifth floor, a high-tech, global satellite-tracking system was installed— the Global Surveillance Center.

Lieutenant General Allen Whitehead, Army Chief of Staff, in his early sixties, short and bald with some gray hair at his temples, raised the lid of a wooden box on his desk and removed a cigar.

"Care for one, Princeton?" he said, holding it in the air. He paused. "Oh, you don't smoke."

Taylor shook his head. He held back the urge to tell his boss to go to hell. Whitehead lit the cigar, stood, and picked up a brown folder. He sat in the chair next to Taylor and stared at him.

"The Secretary selected Matt Brenner to replace Sinclair. Here's his folder." Taylor reached for it. "Offer him the job, and then transfer him from Fort Detrick to DnaTech." He paused to take a puff on his cigar. "The director at Detrick is unhappy. Brenner was one of his best, and he didn't want to give him up. But that's his problem."

Taylor crossed one leg over the other.

"How is Major Wu working out?" asked Whitehead.

Major Joan Wu, an M.D. with a doctorate in microbiology and postdoctoral training in pathology, had been in charge of Biodefense and the biosafety labs for two years. Taylor had her transferred from USAMRIID, the only lab in the DoD equipped to study highly hazardous infectious agents requiring maximum containment at the biosafety level-4 (BSL-4). His assistant commanding officer, Colonel Don Jagger, was in charge of Global Surveillance.

"She's doing a banged-up job."

"According to Dr. Keyes, Brenner's a brilliant scientist. The boss is high on his antibiological." He took another puff on his cigar.

Taylor hated the idea of having the childhood friend of Jack Sinclair in his Biodefense Center. He could be trouble.

Whitehead turned to Taylor. "That damn antibiological is supposed to supercharge the human immune system to fight off any biological the terrorists can throw at us. We need the damn thing."

"But we're still faced with chemical and nuclear terrorism, Allen. We should hit the terrorists now!"

Whitehead scowled at him. "Dammit, Princeton. You know how we feel about that. Don't keep bringing it up."

Taylor felt his heart race. *They just don't get it.*

"Any trouble from Rutherford?" asked Whitehead.

"None."

"I guess not. The son of a bitch is paid handsomely for those two floors."

Whitehead rose, and Taylor followed him to the door. The three-star general stopped, then turned.

"What about that *Red Book*? Any leads?"

"None, sir."

Whitehead shook his head. "I'm surprised it resurfaced. I thought Colonel Osborne had destroyed it years ago. How did Jack Sinclair get it?"

"Don't know," said Taylor. "But Dennis Kugler has it now."

"Get the bastard."

"I assure you, DIA will find him and the *Red Book*," said Taylor.

"No more screw-ups like in Vietnam, Princeton. Make sure you concentrate on biodefense. I don't want Senator Fellows after me again."

CHAPTER FOUR

Matt Brenner left his apartment around eight-thirty that sunny June morning, headed south on Interstate 280 in his Volkswagen Beetle, and thought about what Keyes had learned from Rutherford: the military had taken charge of the investigation. The matter was out of his hands.

Matt had called DnaTech several times, talking to technicians, researchers, and anyone he thought would give him information, even the head of security, Captain Brian Ash. No one would tell him anything. He tried Peter Crane's home phone, thinking his wife could tell him where Peter was staying at the meeting. No answer.

Matt had stopped at a traffic light near the campus when Harriet rang him on his cell phone. "There's a General Taylor waiting for you in the conference room."

"Jesus! We weren't supposed to meet until nine. Does he seem irritated?"

"Not really. He met with Keyes earlier. Better hurry."

Matt darted into the building, threw his keys and briefcase on his desk, rushed to the conference room, and pushed his way in. The two-star general stood by the window looking out. He turned and smiled at Matt.

"Dr. Brenner, I'm General Taylor."

Matt responded with a firm handshake and a smile.

"Have a seat," said the general, gesturing.

Matt pulled the chair away from the table and sat. The towering figure dressed in pressed greens with two stars on his shoulders and rows of medals on his chest chose a seat facing Matt. His strong face, set with deep blue eyes, stared at Matt.

He looks a little like a younger Clint Eastwood.

"I've heard great things about you, Dr. Brenner."

Matt wondered what was coming next. When someone flirted with his ego, they wanted something.

"Normally, I don't visit the sites of people we're interested in, but I had a meeting in Frisco, and since I was in the area, I had to see my old friend, Fabor Keyes." He paused. "Of course, you know why I'm here. Fabor told you we're interested in your antibiological."

"He did."

Taylor unzipped a leather attaché case and opened it.

Matt felt the confidence the general oozed.

"Dr. Keyes' recommendation reached the Secretary of Defense, who's very interested in your work. He would like for you to continue your research with us at DnaTech."

"The antibiological isn't ready, sir."

"Doesn't matter." He removed a sheet of paper from the attaché case.

"Thought the DoD specialized in offensive weapons," said Matt.

"We've changed our mission. We're searching for ways to protect our troops and first responders." He paused. "Terrorists… they have bad stuff."

After Jack's death, Matt struggled with his feelings. Part of him didn't want to go to DnaTech. But there was another part of him that insisted that he go. He decided he had to; no one else seemed to care about Jack. The military treated the incident like it never happened. Now, General Taylor has opened a door for him.

"I'm tempted, General."

"The Army Chief of Staff has ordered your transfer from Fort Detrick to the Biodefense Center in DnaTech. But I had hoped you'd accept my offer before I made the transfer." Taylor paused for a few moments, probably to allow time for his statement to sink in. Then he pushed the sheet of paper in front of Matt. "Of course, we can't force you to go."

No, but you have ways of making my life miserable. Matt decided to accept, but he didn't want to appear too eager.

"Either I go to DnaTech or I am out completely. No USAMRIID. Correct?"

"That's correct. Your position at Detrick has been filled."

"I accept on one condition: that I'm allowed to work only on my antibiological."

"That's the idea."

Matt felt good about the leverage he seemed to have over the military. "Then I accept." He pulled the paper to him and signed it.

The general rose. "In a few days, you'll get orders, airline tickets, and a packet of information. You'll report on July the first."

CHAPTER FIVE

Matt stood in Keyes' office.

He motioned for Matt to take a seat.

"I just left your friend, General Taylor. Offered me a job. Promised me that I could continue working on my antibiological."

"That's what I had hoped. You did accept?"

"I report on July first."

"Good. That'll give you a few days."

"Jack's funeral is Friday."

Keyes paused, appearing mournful. "I'm sorry for your loss. I'm sure the Sinclairs will be strengthened by your presence."

Matt nodded.

Keyes rose and stepped from behind his desk. "Remember one thing about working at DnaTech. You'll be entering a world, unlike the one at Detrick. You must be careful."

Matt knew his experience at the Institute hadn't inspired him with any skills for handling military confrontations, and he would have to play it smart and careful.

"You're a brilliant scientist," said Keyes. "A sleuth, I don't know."

They laughed.

"Work hard on that antibiological. The country will need it."

"I'd like to call you now and then. I may need your help." He knew the old man would be glad he had asked.

Keyes smiled. "Anytime. Anytime."

———— ◆ ————

Captain Ash stuck his head into General Taylor's DnaTech office on the sixth floor. "Got a minute, sir?"

Taylor looked up.

"Dr. Brenner's been making inquiries into the death of Dr. Sinclair. I thought you should know."

"I expected it. Sinclair was his longtime friend."

"Brenner could be trouble, sir."

"DIA's on him."

"Very good, sir."

CHAPTER SIX

Matt glanced at the backs of Eldon and Rebecca Sinclair, Jack's parents, and then at Sandra, who sat next to him in the back seat of a black limousine that followed a hearse into the cemetery. Sandra was five years younger than he and Jack and liked to tag along with them when they were in their early teens. He loved her like a sister.

Matt had arrived the afternoon before and spent time with Jack's parents and the night in Sandra's guest room. They had talked most of the night about Jack, and Matt had promised her he'd find those who killed his best friend.

Sandra had asked Matt to stay the weekend with her parents. Mr. Sinclair was especially fond of him. He appreciated their hospitality, but declined. Des Moines held too many unpleasant memories for him. He hadn't seen his father yet, and didn't know if he would. They hadn't talked since his mother died six years ago.

The limousine followed the winding asphalt carpet through the cemetery, passing acres of headstones and elm trees. Matt caught sight of the white canopy off in the distance.

"There's the plot," said Sandra, looking out his window.

Matt nodded, but paid little attention. He was thinking about the pact that he and Jack had made years ago: they would work together to discover cures for children's diseases. Part of their promise was about to come true, when Keyes had recommended him for a position at DnaTech to work with Jack.

The dark sedan stopped. The funeral director stepped out of the hearse, came to the door next to the Sinclairs, and opened it. They stood by the car, waiting for Sandra and Matt to exit. The pallbearers had lined up on each side of the casket. The director nodded to them to lift the casket and follow him, stopping long enough to allow the Sinclair family to move in behind them, and then they proceeded to the covered gravesite.

Family and friends left their cars and followed the Sinclairs. The minister stood at the head of the casket, while the Sinclairs and Matt moved into the front row of chairs. The minister prayed several prayers and then eulogized Jack. When he had finished, Matt rose and moved in next to the minister and told the mourners that he and Jack had become friends even before they were old enough to know what friendship meant. They were officially blood brothers at the age of eight, and as they grew up together, they knew everything about each other, like a married couple that had been married for fifty years. While he was talking, Matt glanced across the grounds and saw his father standing under an elm, about forty yards away. At that instant, Matt felt like he was slipping into a dream. Words were coming out of his mouth, but he couldn't hear what he was saying. Why was his father standing there? Why didn't he join them? Matt blinked hard from his reverie and ended with an anecdote about one of their childhood pranks. Before returning to his chair, he looked over to the tree. His father had gone. He's still mad at me, Matt thought. Sandra had told him the day before that his father came to the closed-casket service the family had at the funeral home. He left right after. Matt wondered about the closed-casket ceremony. Why not cremation? But then he recalled that the Sinclairs believed the body was God's temple. Fire would destroy His temple, even though He takes the soul from the body the moment it dies.

CHAPTER SEVEN

The alarm went off at six a.m. Matt Brenner rose, sat on the edge of the bed, and thought about what faced him. The seven-thirty meeting with Colonel Jagger would preclude his customary three-mile run, but he figured he would have time later that evening. The nine o'clock appointment with his ex-lover, Joan Wu, concerned him. She could be a problem.

Matt shaved, showered, and dressed, then descended the stairs to the foyer on the first floor, and went into the open kitchen surrounded by a semi-circular breakfast bar with four barstools.

Beechon, a pure-white miniature poodle, met him as he came around the corner of the breakfast bar. Her bottom wagged as she whined and scratched at his legs. Harriet French gave her to him as a reminder of their friendship. He picked up Beechon and held her under his arm as he made a pot of coffee.

"Harriet said you're housebroken, so I expect you to be good." He placed her in the cushioned basket on the floor near the counter, then he slid onto a barstool.

He had arrived in St. Louis the last day of June. Unpacked boxes still remained in his two-bedroom townhouse in the suburb of Clayton. Sipping his first cup of coffee, Matt noticed his hand shaking.

He didn't know whom to trust, or how to go about finding Jack's killers. Taylor's information packet listed Major Joan Wu as head of biodefense research. Maybe she would help him, that is, if she wasn't still mad at him. They had been lovers at USAMRIID, but their relationship turned sour and he went to Stanford to get over her. Then there's Peter Crane.

He stepped out into the warm July air and inhaled. The morning had dawned clear with a light breeze. Matt slid into his white BMW, reviewed the directions Taylor had sent him, and backed out of the driveway. He drove west to Hanley Road, turned south, and passed over I-64/US 40. Tall oaks formed a canopy over the winding blacktop. He topped a hill like an airplane breaking through the clouds and felt a chill. A hundred yards in front of him was a brown brick monolith that could have covered ten football fields. He pulled off the road and eased forward in his seat to get a better look. He remembered reading: one thousand acres with a park, gardens, a lake and oak trees that must have been one hundred years old.

Six stories. He counted them. Mostly tinted windows, except for the two top floors that had no windows. Rows of pipes sprouted from the roof. He pulled onto the road and followed the yellow signs, arriving at a ten-foot, razor-wired Cyclone fence and stopped at the sentry booth. Two guards with side arms in Dress Greens stood outside. He looked at his watch. Fifteen minutes to spare.

A corporal saluted, then approached him, while another guard waved on the cars exiting from the opposite side. Matt pushed the button to lower the window and rubbed the wheel.

"Morning, sir. How can I help you?"

"Here to see Colonel Jagger."

"May I see some identification, sir?"

"I'm Matt Brenner. All I have is the temporary ID General Taylor sent me." The guard peered in at him and looked in the back seat.

"Thank you, sir," he said, taking the ID from him, placing it on his clipboard. Matt watched the guard pick up the telephone, then he reappeared.

"Dr. Brenner, please place this DnaTech sticker in the upper left corner of the windshield. Next time through, you'll need the permanent ID they'll issue you inside."

Just like Ft. Detrick, Matt thought.

"I'd like to come early some mornings. Is that a problem?"

"You're free to come and go as you wish; just make certain that sticker is affixed to your windshield. Have your ID with you at all times."

The guard took a quick step backwards and saluted.

Matt eased his BMW past the booth and waited for the black and white arm to rise. As he drove through, he got this eerie feeling, like he had entered a world that had many secrets.

CHAPTER EIGHT

Matt parked, grabbed the briefcase from the passenger seat, and headed to the southwest entrance. Automatic glass doors slid open, and a massive military figure met him inside. The officer reached out to him.

"Dr. Brenner?"

"I'm Matt Brenner," he said, grasping the officer's hand.

"Colonel Don Jagger."

A six-foot-five African-American male with gray-speckled hair, looking older than his fifty-some years stood before him. Matt gazed at his large flat nose. *This guy must have played football.*

Matt followed Jagger through the bright, red-carpeted corridor; its walls hung with large gold-framed photographs of research and production laboratories in DnaTech. For a second, Matt didn't feel like he had entered a military establishment. On the way to the back, they passed the office of the President and CEO of DnaTech Pharmaceuticals, Inc., Dr. David Rutherford, III, and stopped at one of two red elevators.

"All the biosafety level laboratories are on six," said the colonel. "The Global Surveillance Center is on five." His pleasant smile exaggerated his jowls.

Matt now knew why those pipes rose through the roof—filtered exhaust air was being pumped out of the sealed biosafety laboratories on the top floor. Matt rubbed his nose. An odor of medicine wafted from a laboratory twenty yards from the elevators. They stepped into the elevator, and as the doors closed, Matt wondered why there was only one button in the panel. The colonel's eyes met his.

"Only the red elevators go to the sixth floor, hence, only one button," he said, smiling. "Only way to my floor on five is through security and down the stairs in the back on six."

The elevator doors slid open, and Matt followed the colonel into an atrium. Two soldiers in Dress Greens snapped to attention.

"At ease. This is Dr. Brenner. Let's program him for biometric entry."

"Yes, sir," the sergeant said. He reached for Matt's briefcase and motioned for him to stand at the line on the floor.

Minutes later. "That's it, sir. You can proceed to the sergeant at the table in front of the blue door."

"Here's your ID card," the sergeant said. "You must wear it around your neck at all times."

Matt nodded. He reached for his ID card—the size of a credit card—and slipped the attached cord over his head.

"To enter each time through the blue door, you'll need to look into that box to your right to have your iris ID'd. When the buzzer sounds, you'll be free to enter. Here's your briefcase, sir."

"Thank you." Matt peered into a small box that looked like a camera lens. A buzzer sounded, and the blue door flew open.

"You may proceed, sir," said the sergeant.

Matt nodded.

Matt moved into the corridor. White tile walls and bright fluorescent lights illuminated clean, shiny floors reminiscent of a hospital. He took a few minutes to study the diagram on the wall. The sixth-floor corridor circled an array of biosafety laboratories called Level 3s located in the center of the floor with Level 1s and 2s in the perimeter. In the back was an isolated area known as the Hot Zone, or the Level 4. Next to it were stairs descending to the fifth floor.

Matt joined Jagger as he circled the corridor. Several workers in green scrubs and plastic shower caps stood in the corridor talking and looking serious. They smiled at Jagger when he approached them.

Jagger entered an office and introduced Matt to Rachel Dehart, an attractive brunette with bangs, dark eyes, and dangling earrings. She greeted him with a pleasant smile and mentioned that the major was in the Level 4. He only had time to nod and return her smile before Jagger moved him to the next room.

"This is Major Wu's office," said the colonel.

Matt glanced at the bookshelves around the walls. A side-arm wooden chair faced an executive desk across the room.

"She'll be back around nine. Set your briefcase in that chair."

"I'm looking forward to seeing Joan again," said Matt.

He nodded. "You were friends at the Institute."

We were more than friends.

"There's someone I'd like you to meet in my group," said the colonel.

"Before we do, can I see Jack Sinclair's lab?"

Jagger's big brows contracted. "Follow me."

They passed Rachel and moved into the corridor, passing several labs. "This is where Jack worked," said Jagger, pointing to the door of a Level 2. "Now it's your lab."

Matt looked through the heavy glass windowpane in the door, but it was too dark to see anything.

"What can you tell me about Jack's death, Colonel?"

"An unfortunate accident. He was working in the Level 3 when one of his neurotoxins got loose on him. Don't know how it happened."

"Who found him?"

"Dr. Crane."

"Was there an investigation?"

"Yes. The incident has been reviewed by a panel of officers, and they've deemed Dr. Sinclair's death an accident." The colonel appeared irritated.

Matt noticed the name on the next lab, Dr. Peter Crane. He smiled, thinking what irony.

The colonel slowed his pace at a security checkpoint by the steps to the fifth floor. Jagger introduced Matt to a sergeant, probably in his late twenties, sitting at a desk looking at a series of six monitors on top of six others that showed scenes of the labs and corridors on the sixth floor.

Matt followed Jagger down the steps, thinking about how the colonel reacted when he asked about Jack. He didn't think he could trust Jagger.

The sixth floor was cheerful and bright, but the fifth floor had dark blue walls with dim ceiling lights that made the area into a dungeon, giving Matt an eerie feeling. The recessed doors on each side of the corridor made him wonder if at any second someone would lunge at them.

Reaching the end of the hall, the Colonel pulled hard on the Level 2 door, which sucked air in due to the negative air pressure designed to keep pathogens from floating into the halls. Matt looked around the lab and noticed the same high-tech equipment he had ordered. To his right was a heavy steel door in the wall marked BSL-3. He followed Jagger to the back where a tall, thin man with uncombed, bushy white hair stood in green scrubs.

"Max, I want you to meet Dr. Brenner," said Jagger.

He appeared busy, and he didn't turn around. Matt saw the tightness in Jagger's face muscles.

"Max," said Colonel Jagger with gruffness in his voice.

Max was probably in his late-fifties, but looked older. He groaned and turned his head, staring down his nose at Matt.

He scowled. "I'm busy. No time for chitchat," he said in a voice cold as death.

Matt stared at his bushy white hair and wrinkled face and noticed his shirt was decorated with coffee stains.

"This will only take a minute," said Jagger. "Dr. Brenner's joining biodefense."

Tandenbaum didn't say a word; instead, he gazed at Matt's extended hand, and after a few seconds allowed Matt to shake his wimpy hand, mumbling something.

"Pleased to meet you, Dr. Tandenbaum," said Matt to be courteous, but he didn't mean it. Actually, he didn't like the grumpy old man.

Jagger turned and headed out of the lab, and Matt rushed to catch up to his side.

"Max is either very busy or just not friendly."

"Both," Jagger said. "He doesn't like interruptions, unless he's in his office."

Matt felt like telling Jagger what he really thought of Max, but he bit his lip.

"General Taylor hired him away from the CDC. Max is one lucky bastard. If he weren't such a hotshot scientist, his ass would be out of here."

Jagger took a deep breath to regain his composure.

"Max was an organic chemist in the early part of his career, then switched over to microbiology," said the colonel. "He tells everyone he's a microbe hunter, but that's bullshit. At the CDC he hadn't gone into the field in years."

About twenty yards from Max's lab, Jagger entered into his office and stopped by a plate-glass window in the back of the room, which separated his office from the adjoining room.

"That's the Global Surveillance Center. My pride and joy. Those are special people," he said, pointing.

Four officers—two male and two female—and six enlisted personnel—four men and two women—sat at computers, striking keyboards.

"They're keeping watch over the terrorists' training camps, and their movements in and out of surrounding countries. The Center is a virtual espionage station."

The excitement in the Center captivated Matt. Two-dozen flat monitors and computers were mounted on tables. Blinking lights on maps and wall screens illuminated the area under dimmed ceiling lights. A world map flanked on each side by two large screens covered the front wall. Pictures of training camps filled with trainees flashed on the screens. The colonel explained that the illuminated dots were terrorist camps. Every aspect of the place fascinated Matt.

Jagger moved to his desk and pointed to a chair. "Take a seat." He pulled his leather chair away from his desk and sat.

"I'm not much on military matters, Colonel. At the Institute, I concentrated on my work. I plan to do the same here."

Jagger leaned back in his chair, steepled his fingers like a preacher. "Whatever gave you the idea you'd be doing anything else?"

"Guess I'm just overwhelmed. Don't take this the wrong way, but I feel like I'm in a concentration camp."

"Since the 1993 bombing of the World Trade Center, our research direction has changed," said the colonel. "Research against the biologicals the terrorists can throw at us is what we concentrate on now. That's our primary goal. Nothing else."

"I see," said Matt.

"They're planning something big." He ran a big hand over his face. "Could be a microbe or a dirty bomb."

Jagger's eyes narrowed. He slammed down a fist. "They're insane!" He pushed back in his chair and came from behind his desk. "Let me show you something."

Matt followed him to a table by the window that looked into the Surveillance Center. Jagger picked up several satellite photos from the table and shoved them at him.

"What are these?" said Matt, shuffling the pictures, one behind the other, taking only a few seconds to glance at the body parts in each photograph.

"Innocent people in the Middle East attacked by terrorists. Notice that most of them are women and children."

Jagger said, poking at one of the pictures several times, "Terrorists don't give a shit about anyone. Those victims could have been innocent Americans in Any Town, USA."

Bodies strewn over the ground looked like they had been partially eaten by wild animals. A child's decapitated body, with jagged neck flesh, bothered Matt the most.

CHAPTER NINE

Matt rushed out of Jagger's office, charged up the stairs to the sixth floor, and stopped outside of Jack's Level 2-lab. For a few minutes, he shook his head to rid himself of the images, and then he pulled hard on the door and entered. Illuminated by strips of light from the corridor, the lab had an eeriness about it. He moved in and ran his hand along the wall, groping for the light switch, found a button and flipped it. Fluorescent lights blinked on.

Lab benches were around the walls, with safety cabinets above them, and a biosafety hood against the back wall. Level 2 lab workers handled harmless to moderate-risk agents, those pathogens that have vaccines and are easily treatable. The more lethal microbes were handled in the Level 3s and the Level 4s. These labs required extra protection for the workers.

Matt wondered if someone had wiped down the place. Then he realized that Jack had worked in a Level 3 because of the high risk of his neurotoxins. To his right, a small office behind a plate-glass window had a desk and chair and a bookcase with a few books. He opened the door and entered. He slid the red leather chair on rollers back and took a seat at the desk. Matt shook his head and sighed, thinking that Jack had sat in this chair and worked at this desk. He opened the two drawers on his right. Nothing.

Two rings on the phone disrupted his thoughts. Rachel Dehart, the Center's secretary, reported that his equipment and supplies would be delivered after lunch and that Dr. Wu had assigned him two technicians.

Matt went into the lab to investigate the two doors in the back: one led into a supply closet, and the other opened into an animal room with cages. Not much here, he thought. He then went to the entrance and stepped into the corridor. As he turned to close the door, he suddenly jerked around. His heart hammered against his ribs.

A tall slender man with salt-and-pepper hair had bumped into him.

"You scared the hell out of me."

Sorry."

Matt frowned at the long face with metal-rimmed glasses and neatly trimmed black beard.

"I'm Peter Crane."

Surprised to see a scientist wearing a white shirt, pressed sport coat, and a tie that matched, he said, "I'm Matt Brenner."

"You're the guy with the antibiological."

Matt's brow contracted. "I am."

He looked into the Level 2. "You're moving into Jack's lab?"

"That's right." ☐

Crane must have seen Matt looking up at the ceiling camera. "Don't worry, they can't hear us."

"I tried several times to reach your wife," said Matt.

Crane smiled. "Don't have one of those."

Matt got in Peter's face. "Dammit. I left you messages, and you never returned my calls."

Peter backed away. "Easy. I'm sorry. The major told me you were coming, so I thought I'd wait. Don't like to talk about sensitive matters over the phone."

"What happened to Jack?"

"We hadn't planned on working that evening because I had a concert date. Afterwards, I came to check something in the Level 3 and found Jack dead on the floor. He was in his street clothes."

Peter inhaled a deep breath. "After the shock wore off, I examined his body and found a small hole in his neck. Someone had injected him with the Russian neurotoxin we were working on." Peter ran a hand through his hair. "Jack's body. It was horrible... Oh, I'm sorry. That was thoughtless of me."

"Colonel Jagger told me Jack had an accident—died from one of his agents," added Matt.

"No accident," said Peter. "Bet he didn't tell you the toxin was one hundred thousand times deadlier than the nerve agent Sarin."

Matt became quiet for a moment. Then he said, "Who do you think did it?"

"Don't know. But he didn't die in the lab. Someone moved his body into the Level 3."

"Anything from the autopsy?"

"Nothing. They're spreading lies."

"What can we do?"

"Nothing. It's the military."

Matt understood. They weren't going to expose one of their own, but he came prepared to take matters into his own hands.

"What about the videotape the night Jack was killed? It should show who entered the Level 3."

"Good thinking. Only thing—they've probably destroyed it."

"I'd like to find out for myself."

"That could get you killed."

"Where are they kept?"

"On five. Captain Ash's office."

"Would you help me?"

"I don't know."

"I'm doing it with or without you."

Peter just stared at him.

"We need to talk more," said Matt, "but I've got an appointment with Joan. They're delivering my equipment. Would you mind supervising them and the techs?"

"Certainly."

"Tomorrow, we'll talk research. Eight-thirty in my lab."

CHAPTER TEN

Matt appeared at Rachel's door. She looked up from her keyboard and told him he could wait in the major's office until she returned from the Level 4. He went in and sat in the chair facing Joan's desk.

While waiting, he slipped into thoughts about their turbulent relationship. On their first meeting, Joan told him that her doctor husband, Richard, slit his glove through to the finger on a jagged edge of breastbone during an autopsy on an Ebola Zaire-infected monkey. Billions of the virus infected him, and he died seven days later in the "Slammer," a Level 4 biocontainment hospital suite. His death hit her hard. She buried herself in her work until she met Matt, who came to the Institute six months later. Her depression left her after they had dated a few months, but their romance became bumpy in the second year with arguments, arising from her brother's interference. Kenny insisted that his sister ditch Matt for one of his Chinese friends.

One evening, Joan and Kenny had an argument in front of Matt, and he lost it. He hurled insults at Kenny and showered Joan with words he wished he could take back. The upheaval in their relationship drove him to Stanford to work with Fabor Keyes. They hadn't spoken in two years. Matt was sorry, but feared Joan might never forgive him. He was about to hit a brick wall. Would she sense his sincerity and forgive him? He wanted her... more than anything.

Movement in his peripheral vision brought Matt out of his reverie. He watched as the five-eight, athletic Chinese-American female, wearing green surgical scrubs, rushed past him without saying a word, and then threw a notebook, loose sheets of paper, and keys on the desk and sighed. "Whew, it's been one of those days."

Pulling her chair away from the desk, she collapsed in it. "But you know all about that, don't you Matt?"

He nodded.

As she adjusted herself in the chair, he saw the top of her bare breasts, which told him that she had nothing on under the scrubs. Undergarments weren't worn by handlers working in the Blue suit, a biosafety suit required in the Level 4.

Surprised that she acted like he had been gone for only a day, Matt slid his chair closer to her desk and gazed at the small mole on her cheek. Joan never wore makeup; she didn't have to. Her skin was smooth and healthy looking. Her small nose and shiny black hair gave her a sexually arousing, natural look, which had attracted him the first time he saw her. Matt didn't like women who drank, smoked, used lots of cosmetics, or dressed sexy. Good in sex was okay.

"Your equipment has arrived," she said, moving papers to one side of her desk. "Did Rachel contact you?"

He nodded for a second time, still stunned at her aloofness, like he had variola, smallpox. After all, they had been lovers.

Man she's still pissed, he thought.

"I hope I've done the right thing, taking this job," he said.

She stared at him for a moment. "Because I'm here?"

"Not at all. I just meant that I feel like I'm working under a cloud of secrecy."

"Oh, I see. Different from Detrick?"

"I guess that's it."

"You're slimmer and still look strong. Bet you're still running?"

"Never stopped." Matt smiled, feeling proud of his athletic build. His friends had told him he looked like one of the blond NFL quarterbacks; he never learned his name.

"Your hair is shorter."

He thought about the first time they made love. She told him his sky-blue eyes looked right through her, and how she favored educated men with good looks and strong bodies—and who were good in bed. Hearing he was good in bed had done wonders for his ego.

He took a deep breath.

"Joan," he hesitated, "I want to apologize for the way I acted before leaving Detrick. I thought many times about writing or calling you, but didn't think you wanted to hear from me." He waited for her to say that she had longed for a letter or a phone call, but instead her eyes narrowed.

"I tried to forget that," she said.

He started to interrupt her.

She threw up a hand. "You son of a bitch. I hated you. The things you said to me hurt like hell."

"I'm sorry. I—"

She cut him off.

"Yes, I know. Kenny got between us and that pissed you off. But that's no excuse for the way you talked to me."

Bullshit!

"If you're thinking about a relationship, forget it."

Several bricks fell on Matt.

"Joan, please. I've had time to think. I want what we had before. Believe me, I do." He had the urge to jump up, grab her, and hold her in his arms.

She didn't respond.

"But Kenny... I couldn't stand the way he treated you, always putting you down."

She scowled at him. "It's over between us," she said. "That's what I've wanted to tell you for months."

The whole brick wall collapsed on Matt.

Silence.

He looked at her left hand. No rings. But she never liked jewelry.

"So you're not married?"

"I'm seeing someone."

His gut tightened. "Is it serious?" He held his breath, pretending it didn't bother him.

"That's none of your business." She pushed her notebook aside. "Does the townhouse meet with your approval?"

Stunned by her coldness, Matt took his time answering. "It's fine... I appreciate all you've done for me. I like the area around Washington University."

"I have an apartment near there."

"We'll have to get together some time," he said, to test her.

She didn't respond. He thought it was time to change the subject.

"Joan? You haven't mentioned Jack."

She appeared startled. "That's right... Your best friend. I'm so sorry. I should have expressed my condolences earlier. Jack stayed pretty much to himself." She shook her head. "Unfortunate accident."

Was she keeping anything from him? She never kept secrets from him at Detrick, just the opposite; she usually told him more than he cared to know. She wouldn't lie to him, either, but how could she think Jack had an accident?

"I was at a meeting in Denver when it happened."

"I don't believe it was an accident."

She frowned. "What do you mean?"

"Someone murdered him."

She rose a few inches from her seat. "Are you out of your mind?"

"Why, because I don't believe it was an accident, or because I suspect someone here?"

"There was an investigation and an autopsy. His death was ruled an accident."

"Who ruled? The military. I'd like your help to prove otherwise."

"You don't know what you're asking. I can't help you." She rose from her chair. "Let's go to your lab. The techs should be there."

"Peter Crane and I are starting our work in the morning," said Matt, as he followed her into the corridor.

"Peter's a brilliant virologist. You'll like working with him. Your work on the HIS-mice model is terrific stuff."

"Thanks to Dr. Keyes."

"Did Colonel Jagger show you around?"

He nodded. "We toured six and Jagger's floor. I met Max Tandenbaum."

"Max? What did you think of him?"

"He's an ass."

"He's rude as hell; that's for sure. But he's a great scientist."

Moving through the sixth floor, they met two officers, a major and captain coming toward them. The officers greeted them with a nod as they passed.

"Some of Jagger's people down in the Global Surveillance Center," said Joan.

"I figured as much."

Suddenly, the door to one of the Level 3 labs opened and a tall, middle-aged woman dressed in green surgical scrubs, booties and a plastic cap bolted out, nearly colliding with Matt. He jumped aside. She smiled and scampered into a Level 2 lab across the hall.

Matt pulled hard on his Level 2 lab door, and Joan followed him in. She introduced him to the two techs, Ginger and Melissa. Ginger Layton, a tall slender redhead with big red lips, told them the equipment was functional and that Melissa Graham had started the tissue cultures he had requested. Melissa, a brunette with an attractive slender body, stood by the incubator.

Matt motioned for Joan to follow him into his office.

"What's wrong?" she asked.

"I can see you're still pissed at me, so let's get one thing straight. I won't tolerate any interference in my work. That was my agreement with General Taylor."

She shot him a scorching look. "You have it. But don't think that our past will bend any rules. This is the military, and I'm in charge of biodefense."

At the door, she turned and looked at Matt, and said, "You better be careful… I mean about Jack." Then she left.

Peter sidestepped Joan as he entered.

"The major seemed upset."

"She'll get over it."

Peter closed the door. "Listen. I've been thinking about that videotape."

"Yes?"

"Can't do it. It's too dangerous."

CHAPTER ELEVEN

Max Tandenbaum rushed to the end of the fifth-floor corridor in a coffee-stained white lab coat, no tie, and uncombed hair. He charged up the stairs to the sixth floor and pushed open the door to the conference room. General Taylor sat at the head of the table with his briefcase open, and Colonel Jagger was on his right.

He gazed at them. *Arrogant fools.*

Max loathed the officers in their neatly pressed uniforms with medals and ribbons. He pulled out the chair across from Jagger, who stared at him. The clock over Taylor's head showed one-thirty. He made it just in time, which wasn't one of his strong points.

The general cleared his throat.

"You're on, Dr. Tandenbaum," he said, as he flipped through Max's report without looking up.

The military had learned that terrorists were developing superbugs that could defeat the vaccines stored in the US. Taylor had his researchers looking for antidotes and vaccines for these superbugs. Much of the Center's defensive measures were directed at the Soviets, who had developed a vast program of biologicals from the late '70s to early '90s when the Soviet Union collapsed.

But Taylor had a secret goal: to develop a bioweapon of his own. The most exciting discoveries in biologicals came from gene splicing, and he had Max working to re-engineer an old biological. While his goal was counter to the mission of the Center, and against General Whitehead's orders, he pushed forward. He'd use his bioweapon to decimate all foreign terrorists' camps.

Max began a summary of his work on the inactive Game Point virus. Before he finished, Taylor interrupted him.

"Dr. Tandenbaum," said the general. "All I give a shit about is if the new strain of Game Point is active and if it can be weaponized."

Max felt his pulse quicken. He took his time answering. He struggled with ambient feelings; he didn't like anyone telling him how to do his research, but he felt obligated to General Taylor for saving him after the Center of Disease Control in Atlanta had fired him over his drinking.

Max's temple veins throbbed. "General, you didn't let me finish. Since the Game Point virus was a Level 4 virus before it mutated, we're ready to take the new strain, which I'm calling St. Louis, into the maximum containment lab for testing."

"Now that's what I like to hear," said the general.

"Major Wu can get you trained in the Blue suit," said Jagger.

"No way," said Max. "Level 3 is all I can handle."

The space suits used in the Level 4 were blue, and Max thought any person who got into one was crazy. Hot Zone workers handle the most dangerous microbes in the world, and there were no vaccines and no cures. The major felt comfortable in the Level 4 and even admitted to him that she loved it—seemed to thrive in there.

Max had known workers at the CDC who had gotten into the Blue suit and fainted. Claustrophobia was their major complaint. Others froze with fear when they saw the Hot Zone's latched steel door with its international biohazard symbol.

General Taylor looked at his watch, then stood by the table and turned to Jagger. "Tell the major that she and Sergeant Marlowe will test the virus."

Jagger nodded.

"But she'll press me about it," said Max. "She's pushy and inquisitive."

The general grabbed his briefcase. "Tell her it's a candidate virus that DIA captured in the Middle East. Tell her we need to study its properties to develop an antidote." He paused. "Tell her it's ME-347."

Max looked at Jagger, and then at Taylor. *Where in the hell did you come up with that?* "What's ME-347?"

"I just made it up, for Chrissake. Tell her ME-347 is a lethal virus. Tell her it's a killer; tell her anything."

Max's face hardened.

"If there's nothing more, gentlemen, I'm due in Washington this evening."

CHAPTER TWELVE

Matt jerked. A nudge at his leg woke him around five-fifteen that morning. Beechon pulled at his leg, tail wagging.

"I'm getting up, I'm getting up," he said. His feet hit the floor, and he lifted Beechon to his lap. He kissed her on the head, and she returned his affection with her usual morning lick to his lips. "Whew, your tongue is wet," he said, brushing his hand across his mouth. She wiggled loose and hopped to the floor, turned and barked, then headed down the stairs.

He called out, "I'll be down in a minute."

For some reason, after donning his sweats, he noticed the unopened boxes still scattered about the rooms. Procrastination bothered him. He prided himself in being organized and efficient, but tackling the boxes had to wait. He had more important things to do.

He left at 5:30 for his three-mile jaunt. His Clayton route ended at the famous Rosen's delicatessen, a few miles from his townhouse. Like other runners, he couldn't resist the aroma of one of Rosen's famous gourmet coffees.

Sam Rosen and his wife Janet were in their mid-sixties and Matt learned that they'd celebrated their fortieth wedding anniversary. While they filled his order this morning, he reflected on his failed relationship with Joan. He promised himself that when he turned their relationship around, he'd stay married to her for a lifetime.

Matt moved to a booth with his Hazelnut Crème coffee and sat. Looking over the rim of his cup, he thought about USAMRIID, the Army's lead medical research laboratory in infectious diseases that played a key role in national defense. Joan took pride in that it was the largest biological containment laboratory in the DoD for the study

35

of hazardous diseases.

When he first saw Joan, she was standing in the corridor of the infectious disease building, talking to several coworkers. She smiled at him. Her shiny dark hair and dark eyes accenting a small mole above a dimple caught his attention, and he wondered about her for days. He thought their meeting was a good omen, since he visited her floor only once a month to meet with one of their scientists. Two weeks later, he saw her in the parking lot and invited her to dinner. Their relationship was harmonious until he met her brother. Kenny never liked him. Matt figured out why. He wasn't Chinese.

A jingle from the bell above the door brought Matt out of his daydream. He finished his coffee, waved at Janet Rosen, and stepped outside into the warm sun.

Across the street, people were alighting from dozens of parked cars, and over one hundred had gathered. Large buses began arriving. Two men stood by the curb in front of Rosen's Deli. Plastic badges hung from their necks with their names and *Post-Dispatch* printed on them.

Curious, Matt moved to the reporter whose name badge read Mark Devlin, and asked what was happening. He learned that the group called Citizens in Support of a Better Community were gathering to go to city hall.

"CSBC is meeting with the mayor and the police chief this morning," said Devlin. "They've called for a meeting to discuss the deaths of six homeless men. Earlier, the mayor had refused to provide shelters for the homeless."

"I've heard about those homeless men," said Matt.

"Some of the CSBC members think the chief's glad they're dead." He shook his head. "One of them overheard the chief telling the mayor he had gotten help with his homeless problem."

"You think the chief had a co-conspirator?" asked Matt.

Devlin smiled. "I do. But it's only a hunch."

"The homeless didn't die from poisoning; they were killed," said the photographer.

Devlin added, "The medical examiner said they died of insecticide poisoning from rummaging through the dumpsters, but CSBC thinks the military used them as guinea pigs."

"Yeah. They think the military tested some horrible shit on them, some kind of experiment," said the photographer. "I've heard the Center's developing some nasty shit."

"What's your take on it?" asked Matt, looking at Devlin.

"Mind you, I don't have any proof." He paused. "I believe the medical examiner gave the police chief a cover by lying, and someone in the Center helped the chief get rid of the homeless." He turned to say something to the photographer, who moved across the street and began taking pictures.

"I had a good friend in DnaTech who was found dead in his lab a month ago," said Matt. "I believe he was killed because he knew something related to the homeless."

Devlin frowned. "Dr. Sinclair was your friend?"

Matt's eyes widened. "You knew Jack?"

"Jack told me about a book he had that would expose someone in the Center, but he died before he could get it to me."

So that's what Jack was trying to tell me he had when he called.

"Listen," said Matt, moving in closer to Devlin. "I'm searching for evidence to expose those who killed Jack. Would there be a story in it for you?"

He smiled. "You bet."

Devlin flipped opened his notebook and wrote something.

"Can I use your pen and have a piece of paper?" said Matt. "Here's my cell number." He handed them back to Devlin.

Devlin reached into his shirt pocket, pulled out a business card, and gave it to Matt. "I'll be in touch," he said, and he darted across the street.

———◆———

As he rode the red elevator up to the sixth floor, Matt wondered what Joan knew about the citizens group. She must have read about them. He found it difficult to believe she hadn't suspected someone in DnaTech. Maybe she did, but didn't want to tell him. He had to remember that she was military and thought differently from him.

Rachel wasn't at her desk. He went into Joan's office after tapping on the door.

"About an hour ago, I saw a group calling themselves Citizens in Support of a Better Community, gathering across from Rosens' Deli. Know anything about them?"

She nodded. "Their story was spread over the front page of the newspaper." She covered some details that agreed with Devlin's account of the group.

"A reporter told me that someone in the group overheard the police chief telling the mayor that he had help in getting rid of the homeless. The reporter thinks someone in the Center released something on them."

"I'm sorry, but I don't see how anyone here could do such a thing." Her eyes reflected sincerity. "You want to believe someone here did it, don't you?"

He nodded. "What I've learned points to this place."

"You're way off base, Matt. I'd forget it, if I were you."

"Can't."

———— ◆ ————

Once inside his lab, Matt changed into a blue gown and plastic shower cap and slipped on latex rubber gloves. And met Melissa and Ginger coming out of the animal room.

Ginger smiled. "The vaccinated HIS-mice are doing well, Dr. Brenner."

Melissa Graham added, "The IL-4 mousepox virus is ready, sir."

"We'll be inoculating soon," said Matt. "Thank you both." He walked around the island bench, studying the equipment. The PCR instrument and the DNA sequencing instrument were ready. As he turned to go to the front, he saw Melissa wink at Ginger.

"Thought you could use some coffee, Boss," said Peter, holding a thermos and two paper cups. He followed Matt into his office.

Matt felt pleased that someone called him Boss. He liked it.

Peter shoved a journal to one side to place the cups on the desk and poured coffee from the thermos. Then he took a seat.

"I finished your manuscript on the HIS-mouse model and your designer IL-4 mousepox," said Peter. "Fantastic!"

Matt smiled.

Peter took a sip of his coffee. The light glared off his metal-rim glasses, making it difficult for Matt to see his eyes.

"I'm eager to get started," said Matt.

Peter stared at the slender brunette, Melissa, working at a microscope. "What?" he said, sitting up straight, and turning back to Matt. "I'm sorry, what did you say?"

"See anything you like?" Matt asked, looking at Melissa.

Peter raised his eyebrows a couple of times and smiled.

"We need to concentrate on our work."

Peter shrugged. "Okay."

Scientists in terrorist countries had spliced genes into the genomes of viruses to make them deadlier. Some pathogens had been combined through gene exchange, turning them into hybrids for weapons of mass destruction.

While at Detrick, Matt had turned his attention to the body's defense mechanism—the human immune system—and how it could be used to ward off biological intruders. Since the immune system responds too slowly to subdue bacterial or viral infections, Matt found a way to trigger the immune system to respond with super speed. Since he couldn't test his antibiological on humans, he had to find a surrogate.

While at Stanford, he and Dr. Fabor Keyes developed a genetically modified mouse that had the human immune system—HIS-mouse. This mouse model was hailed by many of Keyes' scientific friends as brilliant. Many substances that couldn't be tested in humans could now be tested in the surrogate animal model. The work of the two scientists also received a slight nod from the FDA, but they still demanded human testing protocols over the animal model.

Matt stood by his desk. "Let's go to work, Peter."

Peter reached for his cup, finished what was left of his coffee, and rose from his chair. "I'm ready."

Three hours later, standing in the animal room, Peter looked up at Matt who had finished infecting the last vaccinated HIS-mouse with the IL-4 mousepox virus. "Good job, Boss."

"In a few days we'll see if the mousepox virus can stimulate a powerful immune response without killing the HIS-mice," said Matt, placing the mouse in its cage.

"Hopefully, it won't storm the immune system and break through," said Peter.

If Matt's theory were correct, the HIS-mice should produce lots of Interleukin-4, which meant that his mousepox virus could be used in humans to protect them against all microbes.

Peter looked at his watch. "Since we're at a stopping point, how about lunch at the Club?"

Matt frowned. "The Club?"

"You don't know about our hangout."

"Should I?"

"The Hawaiian Club."

"Never heard of it," said Matt.

———◆———

Melissa headed to the lunchroom with a bowl of dehydrated soup. She added water and then placed the bowl into the microwave. While she waited, she looked over the room and saw Ginger waving at her from a table in the center of the room. Four other white coats were eating together two tables behind her. Melissa headed to the table and sat facing her. Ginger had eaten half of a ham sandwich and drank from a straw in a chocolate drink bottle.

"What do you think of the Boss?" said Ginger, as she moved the drink beside her plate.

"He's really smart," said Melissa, waiting for her soup to cool. "I think he'll be great to work with."

"I mean, what do you think about his body?"

Melissa frowned. "What's with you?"

"Oh, come on."

"Well, he's handsome and sexy," said Melissa.

"He looks like a jock," said Ginger. "Probably could play in the NFL."

She sipped her drink. "I like those blue eyes and strong face. I bet he's some lover."

Melissa rolled her eyes.

"I think he likes you."

Melissa sipped her soup, taking her time to answer. "He likes the major."

Ginger frowned. "Why do you say that?"

"Haven't you seen the way he looks at her? He has the hots for her."

"Well, he can take me to bed anytime," said Ginger.

CHAPTER THIRTEEN

A little past noon, Matt stepped out of Peter's Jaguar into the bright summer sun and followed him across the parking lot to the entrance of the Hawaiian Club, located in the Clayton's business district. A sail, anchor and fishnet gave the building the illusion of a ship. Inside, shells, flowery leis and pineapples were caught in the fishnet on wooden walls. Business people in suits stood at the circular bar to the left, drinking and glancing at a screen above. Smaller TVs were tuned to sporting events. The bartenders wore Aloha shirts.

On their way to the back dining area, Matt stopped at the buffet to survey the meats, fish and salads. Then he followed Peter to an empty table. The smell of shrimp wafted in the air.

Matt saw Joan and Jagger seated with a heavyset Army captain. At a separate table were three civilian researchers he had seen at DnaTech. Segregation, he thought.

Matt chose the seat facing Peter, who began rubbing his nose. "Do you smell cigarette smoke?"

Before Matt could respond, the waiter appeared with menus. Peter grabbed the menu from the waiter and asked, "Is this the nonsmoking section?"

"Yes, sir."

"Well, I smell smoke." The waiter looked at Matt and shrugged.

"Salad bar and iced tea," said Matt, handing the menu to the waiter.

Peter nodded and gave up his menu.

On the way to the salad bar, Matt saw Jagger nod at him.

Peter filled his plate and returned to his seat.

"Someone's still smoking."

Matt looked around, but didn't see anyone dragging on a weed. He took a sip of his tea, pulled out his chair, and eased into it.

"Jagger and the major are against the wall over there," said Peter, while moving his bread dish to make way for his salad plate.

"I saw them when we came in," said Matt. "Who's that chubby captain with the ugly white mustache?"

"That's fat-ass Ash."

"So, that's Ash? I talked with him on the phone about Jack. How is it I haven't seen him?"

"He's secretive. Got an office on five, but I think he sleeps in his car. He keeps an eye on everyone, especially us civilians."

"Two men in a silver Buick are watching my place. Do you think it's Ash?"

"Could be, or it could be DIA," said Peter.

"DIA?"

"Yeah. Defense Intelligence Agency. It's the military's answer to the CIA."

Matt shook his head. "Does everyone here watch one another?"

"You never know around here."

"I sense you don't think much of the military."

"I work for 'em, don't have to love 'em," said Peter.

Matt leaned in. "I promised Jack's family I'd find those who killed Jack."

He lowered his voice. "Man, you don't realize what you're up against."

"I need your help."

"Did you hear what I just said? Let it go."

Matt whispered, "I can't do it alone."

"And if you find out? What then?"

"I'll go to the police."

"Do you really think they'd go against the military?"

"Maybe, if I had proof." He looked into Peter's gaze. "Or the FBI."

"Searching for evidence is the problem. You'll get yourself killed."

"Peter? You and Jack were friends."

Peter raised his hands. "Hey, don't lay the guilt on me, Boss."

Silence.

Then Peter spoke in a whisper. "Okay, okay. Don't look so damn sad."

Peter's eyes darted over Matt's shoulder, and then a shadow glided over the table. Matt looked up at the colonel.

"How about joining us?" said Jagger.

Matt forced a thin smile. "Another time, Colonel. We're discussing our research."

"Major Wu and I stopped by your lab earlier, but you had stepped out."

"I'll take a rain check," said Matt.

"You got it," said Jagger. He left after nodding to Peter.

Matt frowned. "Why didn't Jagger speak to you?"

"We had a run-in. He asked me to work with Max Tandenbaum, but I wouldn't." Peter threw his napkin on his plate. "Max is rude as hell, and I would never work with him. I threatened to go to General Taylor." He took a sip of tea. "But you could have gone with the Colonel."

"Not without you."

Peter smiled. "Thanks, Boss."

"Now. Are you going to help me get that security tape, or not?"

"I don't know if I can do it."

"I have a plan," said Matt.

CHAPTER FOURTEEN

They waited until midnight.

"You're sure there are no hidden cameras on five?" said Matt in a whisper.

"Positive. No one watches Jagger's floor."

They stood by the Hot Zone lab until the ceiling camera swung out of view, then they sailed down the stairs. Peter knew the location of Ash's office, so Matt followed him as they edged their way through the corridor.

"Here we are," said Peter in a low voice.

"Wow. It's really camouflaged," whispered Matt. "I never would have found it."

Suddenly, Peter pushed Matt against the door in a narrow alcove and spoke in his ear. "Someone's coming."

Matt held his breath. He could feel Peter's heart racing against his back, and the air current from the person passing inches behind them.

Before stepping back, Peter said, "Dammit! You talked me into getting myself killed."

Matt didn't respond.

"All clear. I think," said Peter.

Matt fumbled through a ring of keys. After trying several, he found one that unlocked the metal door.

"Hurry!" said Peter. "We don't have all day."

"Shut up. I'm working as fast as I can." Seconds later, Matt said, "We're in."

"I'll wait here," said Peter

Matt flipped on the miniature Maglite flashlight and entered. Nausea hit him as he stepped inside. He covered his mouth, took several deep breaths, and looked around for a dead body. Instead, he found Styrofoam cups with sour milk and several with coffee-soaked cigarette butts among piles of report forms on the desk. He flipped through a few of them, but found nothing with his name on it. Some filing system, he thought. He wondered if Ash had ever used his office. Then he remembered what Peter had said: Ash mostly worked out of his car.

A metal cabinet covered the length of one wall. The security tapes had to be in there. He placed the flashlight under his chin, twisted both handles, and pulled. They didn't budge. He reached for the ring of keys and tried half a dozen before one worked.

Hundreds of videotapes were arranged on shelves by their dates. He slid a wooden chair over to the cabinet and stood on it, searching the top shelves first, then he worked his way down.

Minutes later, Peter stuck his head in. "What's taking so...? Jesus! What's that smell?"

"Sour milk."

"Smells like someone vomited in here. Hurry it up."

"I can't find the videos for surveillance camera number 7. The last two weeks in June are gone."

"What did I tell you?" said Peter. "You wouldn't listen. Let's get the hell out of here."

Matt slammed the cabinet doors, locked them, and bolted out of the room.

CHAPTER FIFTEEN

Major Joan Wu worked with confidence in a world that contained the most feared pathogens—Ebola, Marburg and Lassa fever, and many others, for which there were no cures or vaccines. The microbes were too small to be seen with the naked eye, and they lurked in flasks, waiting to strike. The environment scared her at times, but she liked the isolation. Constant fear of infecting herself made her overly cautious. One mistake and death was certain.

She and Sergeant Marlowe appeared at the entrance to the Level 4 at seven-thirty. She entered numbers in the keypad. The steel door hissed open, and then it hissed closed behind them. Three chambers were ahead: the staging area, the decon shower, and the Hot Zone, each sealed off from the other by locked doors and negative air pressure. In case of a leak, air would flow into the room to prevent the escape of deadly pathogens. Each room had filtered air pumped into it, independent of the others.

The major went into the staging area first and to her locker, undressed, and placed her clothes in it. After showering and drying off, and still in the nude, she slipped into sterile, green surgical scrubs. Undergarments weren't worn to allow easy movement in the containment suit—the Blue suit. She put on socks, placed a surgical cloth cap on her head, and then went into the Level 3 where she slipped on three pairs of latex surgical gloves, taping them to the scrubs at the wrist.

When Marlowe emerged, they stuck plugs in their ears to block out the noise from the air handlers and from the air that swept over their faces in the biohazard suit. They selected the suits hanging on the wall, which bore their names. He stepped into his, pushed his arms through the sleeves, and then pulled the soft plastic helmet over his head. The wide transparent Plexiglas faceplate served as a shield at the front of the helmet, allowing him to see ahead and to both sides. At a nearby cabinet he chose pairs of thick black gloves that he and the major slipped over their surgical gloves, sealing them at the wrists with tape.

"I'LL GO FIRST," she shouted.

Marlowe gave her a thumbs-up.

She entered the decon shower, an airlock chamber, and locked the door and engaged the shower handle, allowing disinfectant to spew over the space suit for about eight minutes. She turned to the steel door with the international biohazard symbol, unlatched it, and stepped into the Hot Zone. Minutes later, Marlowe appeared.

Coiled red hoses suspended from the ceiling provided fresh air to their suits. Joan reached for one and plugged it into her suit; external cool air flowed over her face. Marlowe did the same, and they shuffled along like astronauts on a moonwalk, passing a "hat box" containing the carcass of a monkey infected with a genetically engineered Ebola strain. It was treated with an experimental antidote, but the antidote failed.

The major had a penchant for developing antidotes and was eager to test the candidate virus ME-347 to develop one. But first, she and Sergeant Marlowe had to determine its effect in the infected animal.

CHAPTER SIXTEEN

Sergeant Marlowe had placed on the lab bench a cage with three rabbits for inoculation. He shuffled along, carrying a test tube of ME-347 in one hand. The three layers of gloves decreased Marlowe's deftness in handling the tubes. As he approached the cage, he bumped into the edge of the bench and the test tube flew from his hand, crashing to the floor, breaking into many pieces.

Marlowe's heart pounded, and his neck veins pulsated so fast that he thought he was going to faint. He moved in the bulky suit as fast as he could to the wall where he grabbed the decontamination kit, sprayed the area with bleach, wiped it clean, and discarded the wipes in a biocontainment container.

Major Wu watched from the next bench. Sweat beaded on his forehead, even though air flowed over his face.

She unplugged her air hose, shuffled over to him, reached for another, and plugged it into her suit.

"YOU OKAY?" she shouted.

"DROPPED THE TEST TUBE. I'VE DECONTAMINATED THE AREA. EVERYTHING'S CLEAN."

She raised a thumb in the air and went to the rabbit cage. Marlowe got another tube of ME-347 and hooked into one of the hoses next to her. Suddenly, both workers froze in place. The rabbits' skin began sliding down their bodies. Thirty minutes later, their flesh was half gone. Sixty minutes later and all that remained were bones and fur in a puddle of gelatinous mass.

"WHAT DO YOU MAKE OF THIS, MAJOR?" said Marlowe.

"SERENDIPITY," she shouted.

Marlowe frowned. "SERENDIPITY?"

"IF IT WEREN'T FOR YOUR ACCIDENT, WE MAY NEVER HAVE KNOWN THAT THE VIRUS GOES AIRBORNE."

She motioned for him to follow her. She unlatched the door and slipped into the decon compartment, slamming the airlock door and latching it. Fifteen minutes later, Sergeant Marlowe appeared from decontamination and began removing his suit.

"Have you ever seen such a thing before, Major?"

"Never." She paused. "It's a slatewiper."

"How can a virus dissolve a whole animal?"

"I have no idea. Maybe Dr. Tandenbaum can tell us."

———— • ————

Joan had called Max and briefed him on the accident. He seemed jovial. That's not like him, she thought. He's usually cranky. She saw he had entered the staging area and went to him.

"Did you say you hadn't injected the animals?" said Max.

"Sergeant Marlow dropped the test tube before we could inject. An hour later, the animals had dissolved into a gelatinous mass."

"Very interesting results."

Why was he so excited over a terrorist's virus that was a slatewiper?

"Well, at least we know ME-347 is an airborne virus," said Max.

"How did the virus dissolve the animals, Dr. Tandenbaum?" asked Marlowe.

"Probably some enzymatic activity."

Max turned to Joan, and said, "You have a phone in the Hot Zone, right?"

"Yes."

"I need to think about this," said Max. "We'll continue tomorrow."

Joan found it amusing that the mean old man would never admit that he was scared to death to put on the Blue suit. He'd probably have a heart attack once he entered the Level 4. Old Max had a kink in his armor, and Joan had an urge to tease him about it, but decided against it.

CHAPTER SEVENTEEN

Joan Wu entered her office and flopped in her chair. She sighed. Despite her love for the Level 4, the Hot Zone drained her energy. Her evening aerobics classes three nights a week had a way of relieving her tension and increasing her stamina. After her husband's death, she'd done little socializing, forcing herself into seclusion— until she met Matt Brenner. Lately she had been going with one of Kenny's friends, but their relationship hadn't clicked. She pushed away from the desk, went to the door, and flipped off the lights.

She looked toward Matt's lab as she left. "Damn you, Matt, why did you come back into my life?"

Joan arrived at her apartment, reached for the mail, and unlocked the door. She stepped in and threw her car keys on the hall table. After scanning the letters and bills, she dropped them on the dining room table. In the kitchen, she made herself a cup of hot black tea and then opened the refrigerator. Fresh salmon was thawing, but she didn't feel like cooking. Instead, she took out the salad mix she had bagged earlier in the week and decided on a salad.

Before dinner, she sat at the kitchen table and sipped her tea. She wondered if Matt ever thought about her or about calling her. Why would he? Not after the way she treated him. She glanced at the answering machine. No messages. What had attracted her to this sexy man? Maybe it was his nice build and deep blue eyes. Maybe she was just lonely. Only six months after Richard's death, she had fallen in love with Matt Brenner. She remembered the guilt. What surprised her now is that she still had feelings for him.

The knock at the door startled her. She wondered who it could be. Her heart raced. Maybe it was Matt. Joan looked through the peephole.

Kenny stood in view. She opened the door, and he rushed in.

"Hello, to you, too," she said, as he brushed by her.

"What's going on?" asked Kenny, standing in the living room with his hands on his hips.

She didn't like his body language or his tone. *Sometimes you can be such an ass, Kenny.*

"How come you told Lee you wanted some space?"

She knew where the conversation was going, and it enraged her. "What do you mean barging in here like a bull questioning me?"

"I thought you liked Lee."

"No. You liked him. And you agreed not to interfere in my life, again. Remember?"

"It's that Matt Brenner, isn't it? You still love him."

Her eyes narrowed. "Kenny. Don't go there."

"Don't get upset, sis. I want what's best for you."

"You liar."

"Mom and Pop want a Chinese son-in-law this time. That American husband of yours... well, he didn't work out."

"You know damn well you turned everyone against Richard," she said, standing at the door.

He shrugged and put his hands up. "Peace?"

"You're not worried about Mom and Pop?" she said. "You're a damn bigot. Matt was right, I should have stood up to you."

"Matt?" he said, glaring at her. "I knew it. You're still in love with him."

She opened the door. "Get the hell out!"

CHAPTER EIGHTEEN

The next morning, Sergeant Fred Marlowe sat on the edge of the bench in front of his locker. He looked up when he heard the major enter. She sat at the end of the bench and reached for a pair of loafers in her locker.

"Are you okay, Sergeant? You seem quiet."

"Lot's on my mind, Major."

DIA had begun following him again, and buried memories from the past had surfaced. As the only survivor of Project Game Point, he had wanted to tell the major what had happened in Vietnam, and who had caused the deaths of his eleven comrades. But if word ever got out, Ash would kill him like he had Jack Sinclair. Marlowe overheard one of Ash's security officers bragging to the captain about how they had deceived everyone into thinking that Jack's death had been an accident. Marlowe suffered from a heavy heart and wanted to be rid of his baggage.

The major had slipped on her loafers and looked up.

"Ready?"

"Give me a minute."

She nodded.

The protocol for today's experiment involved the inoculation of three rabbits with the ME-347 virus and to remove brain tissue to study in the electron microscope. Marlowe watched as Major Wu slipped into her space suit and went to the decon shower. Then he got into his Blue suit.

———— ♦ ————

Forty minutes later, Marlowe appeared in the Hot Zone, shuffled over to the major, and plugged into one of the red hoses. She had the animals ready. They began the injections, and thirty minutes later, they took brain samples before the flesh turned into mush.

"LET'S GO," she shouted.

Back in the Level 3, Marlowe saw the major in deep thought. He asked her what she was thinking.

"I have a theory," she said, holding up the samples. "These will prove or disprove it."

"What theory?"

"That the virus mutates in the rabbit's brain."

To prove her theory, she would have to compare the electron micrographs of the brain samples to those of the ME-347 virus itself.

———— ✦ ————

Later that day in his office, he reached for the phone, but hesitated. Max Tandenbaum took a deep breath. His enmity for Taylor began during their last meeting. He thought about why he even came to the Center. He spent fifteen years in academia, growing frustrated with the politics and incompetent academics telling him he had to become a team player, and the enormous amount of time it took to write grants riled him. Reviewers didn't understand his research, and most attempted to redirect his research objectives. After leaving academia and spending ten years in Atlanta at the CDC, he decided to go with the military. General Taylor made him an offer he couldn't refuse: he could work independently.

But now the general's attitude toward him had changed. The bioweapon was all the general cared about. He would have it, no matter what.

Max lifted the phone. The pressure to weaponize the superbug would become unbearable.

"General? We have our superbug."

"Great news! Great news!" Taylor shouted in the phone. "Weaponize it."

53

CHAPTER NINETEEN

Melissa came out of the animal room. Matt didn't like the expression on her face.

"Dr. Brenner, I think you need to see this," she said, moving back into the animal room.

"Something wrong?" Matt asked.

Peter followed them.

"See for yourself," said Ginger, pointing to the cages.

Matt stood in silence with his forehead resting on a hand over the cage door, peering inside. Peter moved next to him.

"Shit!" said Peter, hitting the top of one of the cages with his hand. "Shit!" He and Matt exchanged glances. "Boss, I'm sorry. I'm really sorry."

Melissa had tears in her eyes, apparently feeling sorry for her boss. Matt circled the cages as if he had expected the mice to jump to their feet. "You know what this means?" He paused, not wishing to broach the subject. "Some country probably has a smallpox virus like IL-4 that would make all the stockpiled smallpox vaccines in this country obsolete."

"Don't even think of it," said Peter.

"I just knew it was going to work," said Matt. "I had faith in it." He inhaled a deep breath. "But we're not going to give up." He forced a smile to encourage his staff. "We're not going to lose hope. Okay?"

They nodded, but weren't smiling.

"I want it understood that no one," said Matt, "and I mean no one, must find out about this until I'm ready to release it."

"Wait a minute, Boss," said Peter. "I just thought of something. Maybe the designer smallpox isn't such a good terrorist weapon after all.

Think about it. It'd probably kill people too quickly and not spread. That makes it a poor bioweapon."

Matt's eyebrows rose. "That's right. Terrorists want something that will spread fast."

Matt paused in deep thought. Then he said to Peter, "Are you ready?"

Peter shrugged. "Ready for what?"

"To shuffle some DNA."

"Boss, you're talking my language."

"Have you ever worked with designer proteins?" asked Matt.

"I did some at the Institute."

Matt had become intrigued with the concept of DNA shuffling in nature. Through the centuries, microbes had learned about eternal life through mutation, the shuffling of genes, to better equip them to survive. The concept of the survival of the fittest was no longer the case. Scientists now believed that any species could have survived its environment by shuffling its DNA unless some external force—like a meteorite or volcanic lava—made them extinct.

"I've been thinking about this," said Matt. "It may take 30 or 40 genes in the right combination to produce the kind of protein I want."

Peter's brow wrinkled. "That means we'd have to shuffle hundreds of genes." He paused before asking, "And what kind of protein is it that we'll be creating?"

"A designer enzyme that will dissolve both bacteria and viruses."

CHAPTER TWENTY

Around six o'clock, Matt reached for his sport coat, turned out the lights, and left for home. The orange glow from the September sunset flashed in his face as he stepped outside of the building. On his way home he noticed the silver Buick in his rearview mirror.

You guys never give up.

At his townhouse, he slipped off his shoes, spent ten minutes playing with and loving Beechon, then poured a glass of white wine and flipped on the stereo. He sat in his favorite chair, sipping wine and thinking about Dennis Kugler's sister.

Earlier that day, he discovered that one of the notebooks on the shelf in his office belonged to a Dennis Kugler. He learned from Peter that Dennis was Jack's research associate, who left after Jack's death, and later died of a heart attack. He had a sister in Ellisville, Illinois.

Matt rose, went to the phone, and opened the *St. Louis Metropolitan Telephone Directory*. There was a Nora Kugler in Ellisville, but no Dennis Kugler.

After three rings, a woman's voiced answered.

"This is Matt Brenner. I work at DnaTech Pharmaceuticals in Clayton, Missouri." He paused. "Is this Nora Kugler—"

He heard a click. *She hung up on me.*

Matt sipped his wine as he paced the floor. He pulled out his road map, went to the kitchen counter, set his wineglass down, and sat on a barstool to begin mapping a route to Ellisville.

What's that? He turned. *There it is again.* A knock came from the front door. Matt slid off the stool, ambled to the door, and looked through the peephole. He jerked backwards. There stood the redhead, Ginger Layton. "What does she want?" he whispered to himself.

"And how did she find my place?" He looked at her again.

"Who is it?" he called out.

"Dr. Brenner, it's me. Ginger. I've got something for you."

Matt hadn't liked the way she had been looking at him lately. Now if it were Melissa, he might not mind. But not Ginger.

"I'm about ready for bed," he said. "Give it to me in the morning."

"It'll only take a minute, Dr. Brenner."

Matt inched the door open, let her in, and closed the door. He saw glassy eyes and smelled liquor on her breath. She wore a transparent blouse with no bra, a short-short skirt, with her midsection exposed. He could see her navel and a red string around her waistline that appeared to belong to a thong. Her red hair was in sexy disarray.

Don't I have enough problems? Matt thought.

They stepped into the living room, and for a few seconds, she didn't say a word. She appeared to be looking at his crotch.

"What is this something you have for me?" *I shouldn't have asked. I think I know.*

Ginger moved in close to him, shoving her large breasts against his arm. A shot of warmth hit his crotch. An erection threatened. He tried to stop its formation by moving backwards. His move didn't work. She moved in closer.

"How about a little fun?" she said with her big red lips in his face.

Her warm breath hit his face. He wanted Joan, not Ginger. But after waiting for over two years, Joan wouldn't have anything to do with him. While Ginger could never take Joan's place, she did look inviting, and he couldn't keep his eyes off her bulging breasts. He had the urge to shove his face between them. The thought of taking her to the couch crossed his mind, but he couldn't take advantage of a woman who had been drinking. It made him feel creepy.

Matt called for a cab and then grabbed Ginger's arm and pulled her out the door. She protested, almost falling down.

"The cab's here," he said as he guided her to the back of the cab. He opened the door and shoved her in. "Don't ever come to my home again."

Then he slammed the door shut.

CHAPTER TWENTY-ONE

As he drove over the Poplar Street Bridge into Illinois, the brilliant afternoon sun raised Matt's spirits. Confidence filled him, knowing that somehow he'd find those who had murdered his childhood friend. Driving south, he kept his eye on the rearview mirror, but he saw no one suspicious. Illinois impressed him with its rolling hills, grazing cows and stone fences—just like back home in Iowa.

Matt entered Ellisville on Main Street. Red brick buildings lined the downtown streets, including cafes, banks, barbershops, jewelry stores, small grocery stores and a Wal-Mart.

Moving into the neighborhoods, he saw two-story framed white houses with porches and swings, large yards enclosed with white picket fences, reminiscent of the neighborhoods in his hometown of Des Moines.

He found Brooks Street and stopped the BMW in front of 2525. He waited until an elderly woman walking her dog had passed before opening the car door, and then he strolled to the porch and up wooden steps and stopped at the screen door. A waft of cooked cabbage attacked his nostrils. He eased past a still swing and peeked into the large curtained window. A woman in a housedress and apron stood at the kitchen stove, stirring something in a pot.

Back at the screen door, he opened it and knocked.

He heard someone's footfalls. The door opened. A woman stood in the doorway and blocked Matt's view inside.

She snarled. "What do you want?"

"I'm looking for Nora Kugler."

She moved her weight from one foot to the other. "Who wants her?"

"Matt Brenner. Who are you?"

"I'm her mother. Nora's not here. Won't be back for several hours."

Matt knew the wrinkled-faced woman with a bun on top of her white hair was lying.

"What's your business with her?"

"I heard Dennis died of a heart attack, and I'd like to see her."

"Who told you that? Dennis isn't dead. He's been sick."

"But—"

She cut him off. "Are you crazy, mister? I don't know what you're up to, but you better leave before I call the police." She moved back, threatening to close the door.

"No, please. I'd really like to talk to Dennis. Do you know how I can reach him?"

She shook her head. Matt wondered if she were debating whether to tell him or not.

"I don't know where he is. Said he was going someplace for his asthma."

"Please. Can I leave a message for Nora?" reaching for his business card. "It's very important."

"What is it?" she squawked.

"I work at the place where Dennis worked. Do you know the company?"

"They make drugs. That's all I know."

He nodded. "It's called DnaTech. I want to talk to Nora about my friend who worked with Dennis. I think the military killed him."

The old woman glared at him. "Mister—"

"Please... I'm telling the truth. Here's my card. Tell Nora I'll call her around nine tonight."

He watched her eyes, wondering if she'd tell Nora. "Will you tell her?"

"Yes! Yes!" she said, as she slammed the door.

Bitch.

Matt returned to his BMW, but stopped and looked back at the house.

The curtain in the window moved. The lady had been watching him. Or was it Nora?

That evening, Matt went to the window of his townhouse and saw the silver Buick still parked across the street. *Still there.*

He placed a call to Nora Kugler.

"Got your message," she said. "Sorry about Dr. Sinclair."

"So you know about Jack?"

"Dennis told me everything."

"I really need to talk to him."

"I don't know. He's scared out of his wits."

"Dennis may know who's responsible for Jack's death."

"I'll ask him. How can I reach you?" she said. "My mother doesn't know what's going on. She thinks Dennis is on a leave of absence for his asthma. It'd be best if I called you."

Matt gave her his cell phone number.

"By the way," she said, "a stout Army Officer with a funny shaped mustache came asking about Dennis."

"What did he want?"

"He didn't say. I told him what Dennis told me to say if anyone in the military was looking for him: he died of a heart attack."

———— ♦ ————

Two nights later, Matt received a call from Nora. Dennis would see him the next afternoon. Matt was instructed to arrive in time to enter a stream of cars heading into St. Joseph's Cemetery for a two o'clock burial and to park among the cars. He should wear a long-sleeve red shirt, but no tie and no coat, and stand by his car.

CHAPTER TWENTY-TWO

Matt maneuvered his BMW into the funeral procession heading into St. Joseph's Cemetery. He turned on his headlights and followed the car ahead of him. Halfway into the cemetery, the cars followed a blacktop road down a slight slope and slowly began pulling to the right, stopping near a row of sycamore trees. Matt guided the BMW to the edge of the road, and slowed to allow enough space between him and the car in front so he could leave before the others. Mourners streamed from their cars like a sea of black beetles, following the pallbearers carrying a bronze casket. They headed toward a white canopy forty yards away.

Matt slid out of the car, stood by the door, and glanced around, but saw no one. Suddenly, he saw movement from the corner of his eye—a man stood by a tall sycamore on the opposite side of the road. Dressed in a long-sleeve red shirt open at the collar, the man looked to his left, then to his right. He appeared to be in his late forties with about a 32-inch waist. He moved past Matt carrying a brown package, and stopped in front of the car, but said nothing.

Matt waited, but when it appeared he wasn't going to say anything, Matt said, "Dennis Kugler?"

He nodded and moved in front of Matt. Kugler stood a head taller and had brown hair. Matt looked into his dark brown eyes.

"I'm Matt Brenner. What can you tell me about Jack Sinclair's death?"

"Can I see some ID?" said Dennis.

Matt frowned, then reached into his back pocket, yanked out his wallet, opened it, and pulled out his picture ID.

Dennis glanced at it and handed it back.

"I came to the Center a few months after Jack."

"Who are you afraid of?"

"Those who killed Jack."

"Who?"

Dennis jerked his head around, but didn't respond.

He's scared out of his wits.

Finally, he said, "Ash."

"I thought maybe it was DIA."

"Oh, you've heard of them. They do secret stuff behind the scenes, too. But it's mostly Ash. He doesn't hide. He lets you know that he's watching you."

"You said, *they*."

"Ash takes his orders from the general."

"The general?"

He nodded. "General Taylor. He's evil. Don't fall for his pleasant demeanor. He and Ash will turn on you like the big cats."

Matt was stunned. He had his suspicions about Colonel Jagger, but not the General. He liked him.

"Why did the general want Jack dead?"

"This," he said, pushing a brown package into Matt's gut.

"What's this?" asked Matt as he juggled the package to prevent it from falling to the ground.

"The *Red Book*," he said, moving backwards. "It'll explain a lot." He turned to leave.

Matt grabbed him by his shirt, pushed him up against the car, and screamed in his face, "I want to know everything you know. Do you hear me?"

"Jesus, Dr. Brenner," said Dennis with outstretched arms. "Take it easy. Take it easy."

"I'm tired of you people messing with me, and I'm ready to kick some ass." He took a deep breath. "So what's it going to be?"

"Okay. I'll tell you all I know. Take it easy."

"That's what I want to hear," said Matt as he released Dennis.

"It's all about Project Game Point."

"What's Project Game Point?"

"A virus gone bad in Vietnam."

"How did Jack fit into it?"

"Someone sent him that book you have and what he read in there really hacked him off. He told some people about General Taylor killing soldiers."

"Soldiers in Vietnam?"

"Yes, and some civilians. It's better that you read the book."

"What else?"

"Ash's men broke into Jack's apartment and destroyed the place, looking for the book." He shook his head. "After that, Jack got involved with some citizens group that fought the mayor and police chief over the deaths of the homeless men. He blamed the military."

"Why the military?" said Matt.

"Jack's neurotoxins came up missing around the time the homeless men were found dead. We both suspected Ash. The military have a history of testing their shit on people." His hands were shaking. "Jack told me if anything ever happened to him, to give you the *Red Book*. I didn't know how to find you."

"Anything else?"

"One night Ash's men broke into my apartment and demolished the place, like they did Jack's." He paused. "They know I got the book, and now they're going to kill me. I must go, Dr. Brenner. That's all I know. Honest."

"Just a minute," Matt said, standing in front of him. "Why didn't you take this book to the authorities?"

"They won't go after a two-star general over something that happened in Vietnam. Even if I showed them the book, there's nothing in there about the homeless men."

"Two-star general? You mean Taylor?"

"He's one mean son of a bitch." He looked around. "Man, let me pass. I gotta get out of here."

Matt stepped aside, and Dennis darted to the edge of the road, but stopped by the sycamore, then turned. "Jack said you had guts. I can see that. Expose the bastards, for Jack's sake and for the others. Be our Watchman."

He disappeared into the grove of trees.

Matt open the car door and threw the package on the passenger's seat. A shot rang out. A split second later, Matt fell to his knees. He glanced around like a soldier in combat, looking for the enemy. His heart nearly hammered out of his chest. It took a few minutes for him to muster the courage to charge across the road. He shielded his body behind the tall sycamore and peeked into the woods. Twenty yards away he saw a body sprawled out on damp leaves, covered in slats of sunshine.

They got Dennis. Matt leaned against the tree, feeling faint. He crouched low as he slipped into the grove. All was still. He made his way to the body and knelt down beside Dennis, who was on his back. Shot in the forehead.

Another shot rang out and leaves swirled like a tornado in front of him. "Good God," cried Matt, as he fell on his face. Would Dennis' body shield him? He inched his head up and looked around. Where were they? He held his breath to make his hearing sharper. No rustling of leaves. No breaking of branches. Nothing.

He had to get away from Dennis. He spotted a well-rounded tree and rolled his body toward it like tumbleweed in the wind. Two shots rang out. One hit the tree; the other hit his ankle. He sat up against the tree to examine his wound. The bullet had dug a path through his flesh. He pulled out his handkerchief, pressed on the wound until the bleeding stopped, then wrapped it. After not hearing any sounds or movements, he sucked in a deep breath and sprinted to his BMW, forgetting about his wound.

———— • ————

Matt sped out of Ellisville, his stomach churning. The image of Dennis lying in the woods seared his brain. *I brought him out of hiding, and now he's dead. What did he mean when he said I should watch 'em, or did he call me the Watchman?*

Crossing over the Mississippi River into St. Louis around four o'clock, Matt switched on the radio and tuned to a classical music station. Feeling calmer, he adjusted himself in his seat and glanced in the rearview mirror, taking note of the cars behind him. His body jerked. A black sedan moved in two cars behind him. *DIA?* He sped up. The black car sped up and moved in behind him. He raced off the Kingshighway exit and drove north. Maybe the police will stop me, he thought. He turned on Delmar, headed west to Forsythe, and then left on Hanley Road south. He glanced in the rearview mirror again. They were gone.

Matt raced toward DnaTech, took the sharp turn into the southwest entrance, and almost skidded out of control. Once he straightened out the BMW, he sped to the guard shack and slammed on the brakes. He inhaled a deep breath, then turned, looking out the passenger window. There it was—parked on the side of the road opposite the southwest entrance. Matt moved into the parking lot, close to the fence, in the direction of the dark sedan and stopped. *Are you really DIA?*

The sedan made a U-turn and vanished. Matt pulled into his parking space, locked the brown package in his briefcase, and placed it in the trunk.

Arriving in the Level 2, Matt motioned for Peter to come to his office.

"You look like hell, Boss. What happened?"

"Dennis is dead. They shot him." He paused to look at his ankle. A small amount of blood had soaked through the handkerchief.

"You're hit?"

"They tried to kill me, too."

"How bad is it?

"Only a scratch," said Matt, examining the wound. "A black sedan followed me as I came over the river."

"A black sedan? That's not Ash."

"Who do you think they were?" said Matt.

"Since Dennis was assassinated. I'd say DIA."

"That's what I thought. They're everywhere."

"What did I tell you about the military? You wouldn't listen."

"Dennis incriminated Taylor and Ash in Jack's death." Matt saw no changes in Peter's face. "You don't seem too surprised."

"Nothing here surprises me."

"He said Taylor was involved in a project called Game Point. Know anything about it?"

"At Detrick I had a friend in the director's office, who told me a molecular biologist, Colonel Osborne, had engineered a very deadly virus that Taylor named Game Point. Taylor got his ass in a ringer for testing it in Vietnam. That was in the early '70s."

———— • ————

That evening, Matt passed Rosen's Deli on his way home and thought about going in for a Swiss cheese sandwich and a cappuccino, but decided against it. The silver sedan was following him since he left DnaTech. He pulled in front of his townhouse, slid out, grabbed the briefcase from the trunk, and darted to the door. The deadbolt lock clicked open, and he pushed his way in. Instead of flipping on the lights, he went to his office, placed the briefcase on the desk, opened it, and removed the *Red Book*. He took it to the kitchen, placed it on the counter, and crept toward the window. He parted the curtains with a finger, enough to peer out. The Buick was parked across the street. Matt licked his dry lips and felt a prickling sensation up his spine. He backed away from the window, sat on the couch, and waited. Beechon scratched at his leg.

After ten minutes, he rose from the couch and looked out again. They had gone. He sighed and moved to the kitchen, flipped on the lights, and took a seat on one of the barstools. He thought about what Dennis Kugler had said about Ash and Taylor: "They can turn on you like the big cats."

Matt's pulse raced as he wondered why Taylor's people hadn't rushed in to kill him. And who were the men in that black sedan? Did they want the *Red Book*, too? He pulled out his cell phone to place it on the counter, and noticed he had a text message from Mark Devlin: *Got some info on people in the Center. Must meet. Police following me.*

He tried Mark's cell phone. No answer. Then his office and his home. No answers.

CHAPTER TWENTY-THREE

Matt grabbed the *Red Book* from the counter and went to his favorite overstuffed chair.

"Let's see what secrets you hold," he said. Thirty minutes later Matt slammed the book shut so hard it popped. He took a deep breath, feeling the adrenaline pumping through his veins. "Those poor souls," he murmured. He opened the book again.

In 1970, Lieutenant Colonel Elizabeth Osborne, an M.D. at the United States AMRIID, engineered a deadly virus, code name Game Point. The war in Vietnam hadn't gone well, and Taylor became excited about using the deadly, non-traceable virus. General Taylor prematurely told General Whitehead about his new bioweapon. The chief ordered him not to use the deadly virus until Colonel Osborne had control over it, since she expressed fear it might get loose and kill innocent civilians.

The new unpredictable hemorrhagic virus killed the lab animals in 72 hours. They had no antidote and no vaccine. She begged Taylor to wait; they needed more data and an antidote. Taylor disregarded Osborne's plea and Whitehead's orders and charged ahead. Eager to beat the other military services in developing a bioweapon, he had a lab improvised in Vietnam and ordered Colonel Osborne and her associates to test the virus on twelve specially recruited GIs—all had been orphans. Volunteers were told they'd be involved in the testing of a new cold vaccine that could be inhaled. They jumped at the chance to participate when they were promised one month of R & R in Hawaii.

Matt leaned his head back.

"We can't forget about Jack, those homeless men, and these

Vietnam soldiers."

He looked at the open book on his lap and read on.

Osborne wrote that Taylor panicked when one of the GIs slipped out from the special medical facility one evening and went to a nearby village to rendezvous with one of the female teenagers. Seventy-two hours later, forty villagers—men, women, children and the GI—were bleeding from every orifice.

Matt saw the story unfold on the screen in the front of his mind. Colonel Osborne had followed Taylor to the village. He had ordered a platoon of men to move in with flamethrowers to incinerate the entire village. At first, most soldiers resisted Taylor's command until he told them the enemy had a fatal disease that could spread throughout Vietnam. Anyone disobeying his order would be subject to court-martial. But one soldier cautioned the general that there were women and children in the village. Another reported that many of the villagers were still alive. Taylor shouted at the soldiers to burn them all. When the soldiers hesitated, he became irate and screamed at them to torch everything in sight, or he would shoot anyone who disobeyed. They leveled the village to the ground and buried the charred bodies in a mass grave.

"The bastard," shouted Matt, rubbing his forehead.

Taylor later justified the incineration to Colonel Osborne as a measure to control the virus. To make certain Game Point didn't spread, he ordered her to scramble medical technicians to draw blood samples from villagers within a twenty-five mile radius. She had the blood stored in freezers, and they observed the villagers for fifteen days. Nothing happened. Osborne and her researchers reasoned that the virus had mutated into an innocuous strain.

Of the twelve servicemen, only Sergeant Sonny Philips survived in an Army hospital in the states. Only then did Taylor learn that Philips had a family. A glitch in the computer had ejected his name by mistake. The Army then listed Philips as "Missing in Action," and then later changed his status to "Killed in Action." His records were expunged, and Sonny Philips never existed. He became Fred Marlowe, a microbiology technician at USAMRIID.

Matt looked up and wondered if Joan knew about Fred Marlowe's background. He doubted it. Turning back to the book, he learned that Whitehead killed Taylor's project. Taylor asked for another chance and promised his researchers could make bioweapons a reality. Thinking viruses too volatile and unpredictable, Whitehead ordered Taylor to increase the research on biodefense—vaccines and antidotes for biologicals known by the CIA to be in the hands of terrorists.

Taylor disregarded General Whitehead's order for a second time and directed Colonel Osborne to genetically re-engineer the mutated Game Point virus. She resisted but succumbed after he threatened her. A note in her journal indicated she wanted to meet with Whitehead, but feared for her safety.

That last page was curious. It had been written in a different hand. Someone had written that Osborne had ripped her space suit while working on a Level 4 virus in the bio lab, and Taylor had her quarantined in a special hospital room, but she died four days later. The last sentence read: *Suspicious circumstances surround Dr. Osborne's death.*

Matt closed the book and set it on the coffee table. He leaned back, closing his eyes. Feeling tired, he eased into a dream state. Swirling in a whirlpool, he fell through the funnel, landing in the middle of a village. He saw a three-foot tubular creature, round and thick like a huge sausage, sucking the blood from villagers like a lamprey, devouring their flesh with lightning speed, and bones strewn over the ground. The creature turned. It had no eyes. It bent what could have been its head toward Matt, dashed toward him, and struck his body like a ferocious animal. Matt clawed at it, trying to scrape it off of himself, but his flesh turned ashen, then cadaverous and melted. He screamed, but nothing came from his mouth. He held up two skeleton hands and tried harder to scream. Nothing.

Matt bolted from his dream, looked at his hands, and pulled on his shirt, stuck to his skin.

CHAPTER TWENTY-FOUR

Max Tandenbaum's ideas on how to weaponize his St. Louis virus were taking him nowhere. He sat on a lab stool, looking around, wondering if he'd ever find a way. The meeting with Taylor and Jagger scheduled for ten o'clock this morning could lead to a shouting match.

———◆———

The meeting lasted fifteen minutes. Tandenbaum returned to his lab to prepare frozen samples of the St. Louis virus.

"That crazy general," he said, rolling his eyes.

Taylor had shouted at him and ordered him to prepare samples of the virus for him. Max grabbed an empty flask and threw it across the room, crashing it against the wall.

"Weaponize a virus? I'm a scientist, not a magician." He shook his head. "He's afraid I'll destroy it."

———◆———

The evening's iron-gray sky forewarned a change in the weather, which didn't ease Max Tandenbaum's agitation as he drove to his apartment.

He skipped dinner and chose to sit at the kitchen table in his small one-bedroom apartment, sipping double-shots of bourbon in coke and ice in a water glass, listening to the music of the big bands of the '40s. After finishing several drinks, he went to the couch. The wind blew hard, and the rain pounded the window. The dreamlike quality of the room had settled around him. The clock on the end table showed eight o'clock. His eyes closed as he laid his head on the sofa pillow, and he gave a sigh of relief. The alcohol had taken over.

As he inhaled a deep breath and exhaled, a wave of relaxation cascaded down from his head to his feet. He had this uneasy feeling he was about to cross over into a dream world. And he did.

Max saw himself sitting at a bar with a glass of bourbon and coke in ice placed in front of him. He leaned his head into his hand, licked his lips, and jabbed at the cubes with his finger. A couple of questions about the St. Louis experiments churned in his mind: Why did electrical energy cause the mutation, and why did the virus go airborne?

He saw movement in his drink that startled him. "What the hell?" A little humanoid dressed in a trench coat appeared on an ice cube. As it danced on top of the cube, it grew larger and larger. He jabbed at it with his index finger. It's the St. Louis virus transforming into a human form right before his eyes. "What's happening?" He looked down at his drink. This time the virus wiggled and danced, removing its trench coat, then putting it back on. It did this again and again— off, on, off, on. What was it telling him? A few minutes later, he shouted, "I know. I know. I have it!" Then he added, "The St. Louis virus changed its protein coat. That's why it went airborne."

Suddenly, the scene changed. He was back in his apartment. The virus danced on his personal computer. It taunted him, waving and swaying like a wiggly doll seen on car dashboards, and then it slid down the front of the computer and disappeared through the disk port. Matt saw his body rise from the couch and stumble over to the computer.

"Where in the hell did you go?" said Max, slamming his fist on top of the computer. "Get out of there," he screamed. A magnetic force drew Max closer and closer to the port. He fought it, screaming, but no sound came out of his mouth. Suddenly, he was sucked through the compact disk port, watching the virus jump from one internal part to another. To his amazement, the virus smiled and waved at him, and then disappeared into the microprocessor chip. He reached for the chip, pulled it loose, and examined it. No virus. No humanoid.

He awoke the next morning when the bright sun came through the window and touched his face. He shielded his eyes with his arm and glided his tongue across crusted lips, lifted his head and his eyes went to the clock on the end table. Seven o'clock. He sighed and lay back down.

After a few minutes, he blew a strong breath through his lips.

"Some dream," he said, looking at the ceiling. He began analyzing the scenes as they played over and over in his mind.

"I have it," he shouted, rolling over on his side too close to the edge of the couch, and fell to the floor on his stomach. He pulled himself to his knees, letting his body rest against the edge of the couch for a few minutes, then rose, legs shaking, stood in place until his equilibrium returned, and trudged into the bathroom.

He showered, dressed, downed a couple of cups of coffee, and left for DnaTech. Max decided he'd tell Colonel Jagger about his discoveries, but not the general.

CHAPTER TWENTY-FIVE

Colonel Jagger stood by the window in his office, watching the blinking lights in the Surveillance Center.

"Show him in, Corporal," said Jagger.

"Max, I want you to see something."

Max stood next to the colonel.

"You're looking at terrorist locations. The bastards are hiding their WMDs."

During the next few minutes, they observed the surveillance experts in the next room scanning satellite photos of terrorist camps.

"The 1993 bombing of the World Trade Center was only their first attempt," said Jagger. "They're planning something bigger." He paused. "What you see in that room is the way of the future for the intelligence community." He turned and went to his desk.

"What can I do for you?" said the colonel. He motioned for Tandenbaum to sit in the chair facing him. The corporal entered with two cups of coffee.

"What's so important that it couldn't wait until our meeting with the general?" He took a sip of coffee and noticed Tandenbaum's bushy white hair and dirty lab jacket. *He's such a slob.*

"I've discovered a few things that I thought you should hear first." Jagger moved forward. "Go on."

"I know why St. Louis mutated. The electrical energy in the synapses of the rabbit's brain abolished the virus's DNA repair mechanism, causing St. Louis to mutate. When the mutant is formed, that same energy in the rabbit's brain stimulated the mutant to change its protein coat, causing it to go airborne."

Jagger took a sip of coffee. "So, what you're saying is that the St.

Louis virus is inactive just like Game Point?"

"Essentially. But that's good. Because it can be transformed into a biological."

Jagger felt a new respect for Tandenbaum.

"Last night a weird thing happened. I had a dream about how to weaponize the St. Louis virus and stimulate it into its deadly mutant."

"Go on."

"Put it in the well of a microchip and attach an electronic board to the chip. Then the virus can be activated by another computer. Just imagine, it could be activated even if it's in another country."

"This is way over my head," said the colonel. "I thought viruses were too unstable to do anything like that."

"Suspended animation gets around the durability factor," said Max. "An electronic board attached to the chip can stimulate the virus back to life when the signal is received, causing St. Louis to mutate into its active form."

"I see."

"When microbes are frozen, they can enter a dormant state and behave like vegetable spores."

"You're talking about freeze-drying," said the colonel. "It's used downstairs in DnaTech."

Tandenbaum nodded. "Once the virus becomes dormant, it remains asleep even when returned to room temperature. It can stay that way for years, or even decades."

Impressed with his science, Jagger said, "You've really thought this through."

Jagger could see delight in his eyes.

"How long does the mutant stay around?"

"Ten days."

"Omega Bytes will spread pretty far in ten days. We'll need Dr. Brenner's antidote."

"Without it, Omega Bytes can't be controlled," said Max.

The colonel finished his coffee. "The beauty of your invention is that no one would ever suspect the computer as a bioweapon."

"And it can't be traced to the US," said Max. "The devastation can be blamed on some radial group."

"When will the chip be ready?"

"I'm meeting with my group tomorrow."

As he eased backwards in his chair, Jagger stared at his family picture on the desk for a few minutes.

Tandenbaum rose.

"Wait a minute," said the colonel. "I've not seen the results of the rabbit test."

"Omega Bytes dissolved the rabbits in sixty minutes. Only fur and bones were left in a gelatinous mass."

"You're shitting me? You mean a slatewiper?"

"Slatewipers kill about ninety percent of their victims," said Max. "Omega Bytes will kill one hundred percent."

CHAPTER TWENTY-SIX

Matt drove through the light rain to make his appointment with Police Chief Brewer. He fumed about what Taylor had done in Vietnam and about Dennis Kugler alleging that Taylor had Jack killed.

About four miles from the station, Matt blinked out of his thoughts. Shocked that he was about to ram the back of an 18-wheeler, he swerved to his right, losing control of the BMW. It flew between two parked cars, hopping the curb and landing on the sidewalk, halting a few inches from a brick wall. Adrenaline pumped through his veins.

He inhaled a deep breath, backed away and drove off. "What else is going to happen?"

He rolled up to the next intersection and stopped at the traffic light, still aware of his racing heart, pulsating in his ears. He rubbed his hands around the steering wheel.

"Get hold of yourself."

He steered the BMW through the entrance of the parking lot and found a spot on the side of the building toward the front, next to a police car, and moved in. When he exited the car, two uniformed policemen came towards the police car parked next to his; one passed him and slid into the front seat on the passenger side.

Matt negotiated the concrete steps in front of the entrance, cleared the top step, and yanked open the heavy glass door. Standing inside, his mouth went dry and his hands felt clammy. He glanced over the capacious room. Lofty ceilings with fluorescent lights reflected brightness throughout. He could have seen a bull's-eye fifty yards away. He grabbed the arm of the detective closest to him—a short thin man with a white shirt opened at the collar, rolled up sleeves, loose tie, and wrinkled pants. He looked like he hadn't slept in days.

The detective frowned and pulled his arm away.

"Chief Brewer?" said Matt.

Without looking at him, the detective pointed toward a series of glass-enclosed offices in the back, hung with Venetian blinds. Matt edged his way through the detectives and stopped by two uniformed officers, drinking coffee from Styrofoam cups and eating Krispy Kreme donuts.

"Chief Brewer?" said Matt.

The larger officer stared at him while he took a sip of coffee, then asked, "What's the name?"

"Matt Brenner. He's expecting me."

The officer turned, adjusted his gun belt, and went to the back. He knocked on the door, opened it, and entered without closing it. Matt heard his name mentioned. Moments later, the officer reappeared, motioning for Matt to go in. On the way Matt saw the lettering on the window of an adjacent room—"Interview Room #1." The blinds were open. It was empty.

Entering the chief's office, Matt regarded the large man with a round face and crew cut who rose from his desk. Matt thought the fifty-year-old, six-foot law enforcement officer looked as big as a refrigerator.

"Chief Brewer," he said. "How can I help you, Dr. Brenner?"

Matt shook his hand and said, "I'm here about the homeless men who died a few months ago, and about a friend of mine, who I believe was murdered in the Biodefense Center at DnaTech."

"Take a seat," said the chief, gesturing. He sat and rested his bulging arms on the desktop.

Matt settled in the chair by a small table in front of the chief's desk, and explained that three biological agents were stolen from Jack's lab, and that Jack knew the Army had tested them on the homeless, that's why he was killed. "I think an investigation is in order, since the homeless deaths occurred in the city and not on any military installation."

"Just a minute, Dr. Brenner," said the chief, "I investigated those deaths myself. Those men died from pesticide poisoning from rummaging through dumpsters. We have witnesses who saw them, and the medical examiner said the shit was absorbed through their skin. Autopsies proved it."

"Someone's not right, Chief. My friend told me they died from neurological damage, not pesticide poisoning."

Brewer's eyes narrowed. "Your friend was wrong."

"Then what about my friend? He was a civilian working for the Army in the Center, and someone injected him with one of his neurotoxins. As a civilian, his death should warrant an investigation from the civilian authorities."

The chief's thick neck muscles tightened. He came from behind the desk and opened the door.

"All that is military business. Take it up with them."

Matt rose and passed in front of the big man whose face was as red as watermelon meat. He saw a killer's instinct in the eyes of the chief.

Too bad your mother didn't have an abortion, Matt thought, as he left and edged his way through the throng of detectives who were laughing at him. Before he reached the front door, an officer sitting close to the door smiled and nodded at Matt. His eyes sent a message: *He's the one.*

Matt left the building, entered his car, and slammed the door. He rested his head on his hands, as he gripped the steering wheel.

Seconds later, he lifted his head and looked around. His knuckles were white.

"I'm over my head in this."

He drove through the exit and pulled out of the parking lot, heading west toward Clayton. About to pass the car in front of him, he glanced into the rearview mirror. A dark sedan had turned the corner and moved in two cars behind him. The silhouette of the two men in the front looked like those who had followed him from Ellisville. He had expected the silver Buick.

He kept an eye on the rearview mirror and side mirrors as he maneuvered through the side streets in Clayton. He pulled into the back lot of Rosens' Deli and stood by his BMW, watching the cars that passed by on Hanley Road. The dark sedan wasn't one of them.

———— ◆ ————

Chief Brewer grabbed the phone and called General Taylor.

"General? This is Chief Brewer. Matt Brenner was here asking for an investigation into the deaths of the homeless. He also wanted me to look into the death of Jack Sinclair." The chief snorted. "General, Brenner said he had evidence."

"You worry too much, Chief. We'll take care of him in due time."

"Maybe we should scare him a little," said the chief, "so he'll back off."

"Negative. Negative!"

A pause.

"Listen, General... about the homeless—"

The general cut him off. "We took care of that problem for you," said the general. "Now you keep your end of the bargain."

"And we'll take care of that *Post-Dispatch* reporter for you... and that will make us even. But if it ever gets out about the homeless, it'll—"

"I said, we'd handle Brenner!" His voice took on an impatient edge. "Sit tight and keep your damn trap shut."

———— ✦ ————

Matt hadn't had time for his run this morning, so he decided to head out after work to run off his frustrations. When he returned, he ran through his cooldown in the park across from his townhouse. The sun had set, and he could barely see across the street. Running in place by several evergreen bushes, Matt felt a blow to the head, and he fell on his face. Next thing he knew, someone was kneeling beside him. He started to cry out, but froze. The barrel of cold steel was shoved against his neck.

"You nosy son of a bitch. Keep away from Mark Devlin."

Then Matt heard retreating footsteps and a car squealed away.

"Damn," said Matt, rubbing his head as he got to his knees.

Something warm trickled down on his ear, and he could taste blood. Car headlights passed, and people were looking out their windows from across the street. An old man walking his dog through the park stopped and asked, "Are you okay, mister?"

"Just fell, but I'm okay. Thanks."

CHAPTER TWENTY-SEVEN

With headlights off, he inched the BMW into the empty waterfront lot next to the Gateway Arch, away from the streetlights, parked, turned off the engine, and waited. The rain had stopped, and the sky was black. He chose a good night, thought Matt. A breath later, he saw it. A black sedan crept in front of his car and pulled into the space next to him.

Matt waited. He saw the burst from a cigarette lighter. He opened the car door and climbed out. The rear door of the sedan opened, and Matt slid in. Two men were in the front seat. One in the back. All dressed in black suits.

"Special Agent Cousins?" asked Matt.

"Yes," said the man next to him.

In the dim light, Matt could see his round face and the whites of his eyes. He had a thin beard and dark hair.

"Why are we meeting like this?"

"DIA."

"I know about the DIA," said Matt. "But you're FBI."

"Doesn't matter. There are fourteen other intelligence agencies, and we watch each other."

"Does meeting like this have anything to do with the Center?"

"It does," said Agent Cousins.

"And General Taylor's DIA?" said Matt.

"He's the head of it."

Matt had gotten Cousins' name from Detective Purvis of the Palo Alto Police Department. Chris Cousins was a Special Agent in the FBI SLFO, or St. Louis Field Office. During his telephone conversation with Cousins, Matt asked for his help to find those who killed Jack Sinclair. He explained that Police Chief Brewer threw him out of his office, and he couldn't go to the military because they were involved.

"How'd you get those scratches on your face?"

"Last night, after my run, I was cooling down in the park across from my place, when someone clobbered me and shoved a gun in my neck, told me to stay away from the *Post-Dispatch* reporter Mark Devlin."

"Obviously, the reporter's on to someone," said the agent.

Matt nodded. "That's what I thought."

"On the phone you said you have evidence," said Cousins.

Matt told him about Jack's telephone call, about his stolen biologicals, and how they were used against the homeless. That he had met with Dennis Kugler who gave him the *Red Book*. That he believed General Taylor ordered Jack killed because Jack was going to expose him for testing the biologicals on the homeless men, and for the things he did in Vietnam.

"You should think about giving up that book," said Cousins.

"You mean in case I'm gunned down?"

"It's evidence we can use."

"So, you know about the book, too?"

The agent didn't respond.

Of course you do. Matt paused, thinking the FBI could have protected Dennis. But why didn't they?

"Was the FBI ever interested in Dennis Kugler?" said Matt.

"We were watching him."

"Who got him?" asked Matt.

"DIA," said Agent Cousins.

"I had thought Ash and his men."

"Ash is too sloppy," said the agent in the passenger seat. "He couldn't hit the side of a barn."

"DIA tried to kill me," said Matt.

"Hitting you in the foot was just a warning," said the agent behind the steering wheel. "They could have easily taken you out, if they wanted to."

Matt looked at Cousins. "Is that right, Special Agent Cousins?"

"The name is not Special Agent Cousins. It is Chris. And yes, they could have. Easily."

"Why didn't they?"

"Taylor must need you for some reason."

My biological, thought Matt.

"Wait a minute," said Matt. "How in hell did you know I was hit in the foot? I didn't mention it." He paused for a moment. "You bastards were there, weren't you?"

Chris didn't respond.

"You had to be. Probably watching Dennis." He paused. "Why didn't you stop them?"

No one responded.

Some interagency thing, Matt thought, spying on each other. It was all bullshit to him.

"You must have radioed ahead to have me followed after I got back into St. Louis."

Chris said, "We're interested in you, Dr. Brenner."

"Oh, so now it's Dr. Brenner. I guess I should have guessed; you have a file on me, too. Well, it's not Dr. Brenner. It's Matt."

"We know about everyone in the Center," said Chris.

"Are you going to help me? Or does this mean there has to be a tradeoff?"

"Sort of. We need your help."

"Now that's a twist. The FBI needs my help."

"General Taylor's involved in a group called APAT, American Patriots Against Terrorists, along with its leader, known only as Mors."

"Never heard of APAT or Mors."

"They're an ultra-conservative organization, fanatical and dangerous. They've taken the position that the FBI is incompetent and can't handle Homeland Security, so they're planning on doing it."

Matt had read several articles about the problems in the FBI and CIA. They didn't like to exchange information. It was all about ego, control and budget. Both agencies have their prima donnas, thought Matt.

"So how does APAT plan on protecting this country?"

"Capture and execute terrorists."

"Jesus. That's scary. That makes them terrorist."

"You're getting the gist of it."

"Are you sure about Taylor and this Mors fellow?"

"An informant had a document that could have exposed APAT."

"You didn't get it?"

"Someone assassinated him before we got it."

"DIA?"

"No, APAT."

"What did they do to him?"

"Ran him off the road in a high speed chase. Crushed his car flatter than a pancake."

Matt flinched. Being crushed in car was akin to dying in a tomb. "Who was the informant?"

"Someone in the military."

"With that document, you could have arrested APAT."

"We need to learn all we can about the organization and who's in it, before we can do anything. And that's where you come in."

"How?"

"Gathering information on Taylor and Mors."

Before Dennis Kugler and the *Red Book*, Matt never thought Taylor was a bad guy. Maybe because he was seldom around. He did wonder about Jagger, though.

"What do I have to do?"

"Here's my secure number," said the agent, as he handed Matt a card.

Matt put it in his shirt pocket.

"Memorize the number, and then destroy it. I'll be in touch with you."

Matt nodded, and then opened the door.

"One other thing," said Chris, "you might think about giving me that *Red Book*."

CHAPTER TWENTY-EIGHT

The next evening, Matt strolled to the entrance of his townhouse, but stopped before entering. The door was ajar. He remembered locking it this morning. *Someone's in there.* For a few seconds he debated whether to call 911 or Chris Cousins. He pulled his cell phone from his pocket and called Chris, who told him not to go in. To wait for him.

Matt eased the door open. Then stopped. His pulse quickened as he stepped inside the foyer; he moved to the banister to his right, glanced up the stairs, and listened. No sounds. No movement. He went to the edge of the living room. His heart pounded.

Books were strewn over the floor, drapes torn from the windows, and the rug ripped from the floor. He eased in and glanced into the kitchen. The refrigerator door was open, and cabinet drawers and utensils were on the floor.

Matt flipped around, almost wetting his pants.

Chris held an index finger against his lips, then moved past him with his Glock gripped in both hands, arms extended, waving them from side-to-side, as he checked each room. Then he went to the stairs with his Glock still extended in front of him, elbows locked, and ascended the stairs.

A few minutes later, he descended the stairs and said, "All clear." He shook his head. "They really wrecked the place. Cut through your mattresses. Clothes and shoes are everywhere."

Chris moved in front of Matt. "I told you to wait. If I were one of them, you'd be dead."

Matt knew Chris was right, but how could he have waited. Someone broke into his home and scattered his things. He felt violated. Like they'd exposed his secret world.

He followed Chris into his office. Books and journals from the wall shelves were scattered on the floor. Contents from the desk drawers were strewn about. Both computer and monitor had been crushed.

"The hard drive is missing." Chris looked around the room. "See anything missing that you haven't told me about?"

Matt shook his head. "Nothing."

"It's obvious they were after the *Red Book*," said Chris.

"You mean DIA?"

"This is more like what Ash would do," said Chris. "It's time to turn it over to me."

"It's not here," said Matt. "I'll let you know."

"Trust me."

They moved into the living room, and Matt went to the fridge to get a bottle of water. As he closed the door, he dropped the bottle and fell to his knees. Beechon lay on the floor next to the cabinet. During the excitement, he had forgotten about her.

"Beechon," he cried, as he picked her up. Her head dangled over his arm, tongue clamped between her teeth. "What have they done to you?"

Tears trickled down Matt's face.

Chris rushed to the counter.

Silence.

Matt hugged her and said, "Baby Girl, you're the only one who really cared about me."

———◆———

"Ash here," said the Security Captain.

"The book wasn't in Brenner's place," one of his men said.

"Dammit," said Ash, slapping his hand on the desk. "We have to find that book. The general's on my ass about it."

"Should we do a Sinclair on Brenner?"

"Are you crazy!"

Ash broke the circuit and dialed the number for General Taylor.

"What is it, Brian?" said Taylor.

"The book wasn't in Brenner's house. Do you want us to take care of him?"

"Negative. Negative. I have something special planned for Dr. Brenner, but not until I get his antibiological."

CHAPTER TWENTY-NINE

Matt pulled into the parking lot at Washington University, left his car with briefcase in hand, and went to the concrete stairway. He climbed the fifty-some steps, thinking about how no one would ever miss the eleven Game Point volunteers. Puff. They're gone. And what about what Taylor did to Jack and the homeless men and now Dennis?

Reaching the top, he passed through the arch and went to the library at the west end of the quadrangle, pushed his way through a large glass door, and stepped inside. A scent reminiscent of his days in the library drifted to him and settled in his nostrils. An odor he attributed to the glue in the books.

Chris sat at a table in the back, and Matt strolled down the center aisle, passing hordes of students spread out among dozens of tables. Some were talking, and others had their noses in books. Many had earphones plugged in. Matt caught snatches of musical tunes as he passed them.

This was the first time he got a good look at Chris. The other night he was too scared to regard him. Chris had big brown eyes, which was the first thing Matt noticed about him. They went well with his healthy, round face and dark brown hair. When he smiled, his eyes smiled also. Apparently, he liked wearing suits, and his broad shoulders gave him a professional look, like a businessman.

Matt placed his briefcase on the table, opened it, and threw the *Red Book* in front of him.

"It's a time bomb ready to go off," said Matt. "Don't need it anymore."

"Smart move," said Chris, placing the book in the leather satchel on the chair beside him.

"What will DIA do now?" asked Matt.

"Don't believe Taylor'll involve them. It's Ash's turn. He'll do whatever the general wants him to do. But we'll keep an eye on him." Chris reached into his satchel, pulled out a cell phone, and handed it to Matt.

"I have one," said Matt.

"Take this one. It's secure."

Matt reached for the phone and put it in his coat pocket.

"We need those documents as soon as possible."

"I'm ready," said Matt.

———————◆———————

On his way to DnaTech, Matt stopped at a traffic light, thrust a hand into his coat pocket, and snapped up the cell phone Chris had given him and dialed the number for Keyes at Stanford. While waiting for the light to change, Matt realized how much respect he had for him. Keyes always knew what to do. He was like a surrogate father. The stoplight changed, and Matt sped through the intersection with the phone pressed against his ear. Seconds later, Keyes answered. Matt began telling him about Project Game Point and briefly covered the contents in the *Red Book*.

Matt could hear Keyes breathing hard in the phone.

"I am shocked to hear this about Princeton," said Keyes. "I have known him a long time, and wouldn't have guessed that about him."

"He's also involved in an organization called APAT. Have you heard of them?"

Keyes took his time answering. "APAT? No. I never heard of them."

"What about Mors?" said Matt. "He's their leader."

"Can't say that I've ever heard of that name either."

"Thanks, sir. I just wanted to run this by you."

"Matt…" He could hear the pain in his mentor's voice.

"Sir?"

"Be careful."

"Thank you, sir. I will."

He closed the phone. Just hearing the old man's voice made him feel better.

Back at his office, Matt sat at his desk wondering if Peter had ever heard of Elizabeth Osborne. He confronted Peter and was shocked to learn that he knew about the *Red Book* and Dr. Osborne.

"Why didn't you tell me Jack had the book?"

"At the time we discussed Game Point, I thought that was enough."

Matt felt betrayed. "I trusted you. You should have told me everything."

"At the time, I misjudged your passion for finding Jack's killers. I thought it'd blow over."

Matt was confused. Peter knew about the book, yet he wasn't in any apparent danger. Why did Peter think he had to protect him?

"So you wanted to protect me?"

"I thought, like Jack, you might talk too much in your quest for the truth. How did I know?"

The APAT informant's demise flashed into Matt's mind. The FBI couldn't protect him every minute, and his own demise could come at any time, any place—in the lab or on the street.

"Have you ever heard the name Mors?" said Matt.

Peter shook his head. "No, why?"

"Not important."

Peter stood up. "Be careful who you talk to, Boss."

"I plan to."

Matt rose, went into the corridor, and stepped into Rachel's office. "Is she in?"

Her eyes smiled at him, as she said, "Go right in, Dr. Brenner."

———◆———

Joan looked up when Matt tapped at the door. He moved in and stood by the chair. She noticed a worried look on his face. She waited for him to say something, but he only gazed at the gold-frame picture of an aerial view of USAMRIID, hanging on the wall behind her.

"Nice picture," he said.

"You hadn't noticed it before? The general gave it to me."

He shrugged. "I've got something to tell you."

He outlined Project Game Point, Taylor's role in it, and the massacre in the Vietnamese village. Joan held her hands together, fingers up against her lips, staring at him while he spoke.

When he finished, she asked, "How do you know all that?"

"Did you ever hear of a Colonel Osborne at Detrick?"

"I knew she worked there before me. What about her?"

"She kept a journal called the *Red Book*. Ever hear of it?"

Joan's brow rose. "And you have it?"

He said nothing. Just stared at her.

He has it, she thought.

"Did you know that Sergeant Marlowe was the only survivor of Game Point and that Fred Marlowe isn't his real name? It's Sonny Philips."

Joan fell silent. *I can't believe what I'm hearing.* Then she said, "He never mentioned it."

"Maybe he doesn't trust you."

Joan scowled at him. "What the hell are you saying?"

"Who do you think mistreated him, the Navy?"

She didn't respond.

"All I'm saying is: I find it hard to believe that you being a major and close to the brass that you didn't hear anything."

"Damn you. What do you want from me?"

"The truth."

"Does this mean you don't trust me?"

"Would I tell you this, if I didn't trust you?" he said. "How do you feel, knowing what General Taylor did in Vietnam?"

"At the moment, I'm not making any judgment calls." She could have strangled Matt, questioning her like a child.

Matt crossed one leg over the other. "Then what about the six homeless men?"

Where is he going with this, she thought. "I don't know what you mean."

"How do you think they died?"

"Insecticide poisoning from rummaging through dumpsters. That's what the paper said."

"You believe everything you read?" said Matt.

"I have no reason not to."

"I have a theory."

"And…?"

"Someone in the Center deliberately tested biologicals on them."

"Here we go again. So you think it was the general?"

He nodded. "Let's say the homeless men were used as human guinea pigs—"

She interrupted him. "He couldn't pull that off. The ME would have discovered the biological."

"Not if he were a co-conspirator."

"What about the police?" she said.

"Co-conspirator."

"Why?"

"I don't know yet."

"What about my friend Jack Sinclair?" asked Matt. "You said he had a lab accident."

"All evidence pointed to an accident."

"Trumped-up evidence."

He told her Peter had found Jack with a neck puncture, caused by an injection. "We believe Taylor and Ash are involved in all the killings."

Joan thought about all he had said. "Of course, I'm against human testing, and those who did such a thing should be brought to justice. But you must have proof." She paused. "Anyway, the general stopped human experimentation after Senator Fellows' investigations."

"Don't be naive," said Matt. "The military has this huge wall of secrecy surrounding it. No one outside can see what the military is doing. That's why they'll get away with the deaths of Jack and the homeless, if we don't do something."

"Loyalty," she said, "that's how they get away with it. The military disdains snitches. It's a fraternity."

"Will you remain loyal now that you know what Taylor's done?"

She frowned. "I'm obligated to my conscience. You know it'll be hard to get any evidence against him."

"We'll get it."

CHAPTER THIRTY

The Joint Chiefs and the Directors of the CIA and FBI arrived in the Situation Room of the Pentagon a few minutes before the scheduled nine-o'clock briefing. They had already taken their seats before Taylor had arrived. Taylor, head of the Defense Intelligence Agency, chose a seat across from his boss, Lt. General Whitehead, the Army Chief of Staff, who held an unlit cigar in his hand.

Rear Admiral Bob Meacham, Chairman of the Joint Chiefs, was a stickler for everything, but not for starting on time. Taylor knew the Chairman didn't like him, since he had opposed him on several defense measures.

Meacham sat at the front of the long executive table with the CIA and FBI Directors on each side of him. Taylor looked around the gray room clouded with acrid tobacco smoke, maps on the wall, and a mahogany table with twelve red-leather chairs. A room of gloom and doom, he thought.

Meacham opened the meeting by thanking the Directors for coming and stated that the CIA Director would speak first, followed by the FBI Director. The CIA Director told the group about a serious buildup of terrorists in the Middle East. Several large cells of Islamic extremists were being trained in terrorist tactics and germ warfare. The network extended into many countries, primarily in Egypt, Afghanistan and Pakistan. The al-Qaeda, 'the base,' the Islamic Army, and the World Islamic Front for Jihad Against Jews and Crusaders were the most troublesome. Intelligence had secured documents that defined a plan to infiltrate many US cities and establish cells. To date, there were thirty-six terrorist organizations in the network.

Taylor eased forward in his chair, feeling his muscles tighten and his ears ringing. He wanted to shout: *Annihilate them before they slip into this country, you dumb shits.*

"You have something to say, General Taylor?" said Meacham.

"Sir, the terrorists should be stopped dead in their tracks, or they'll sneak into this country again." He paused. "Remember four years ago, the 1993 World Trade Center?" He stood up. "I tell you they'll be back."

"Let's wait until we hear from the FBI director, then we can discuss it," said the admiral.

Taylor nodded and looked at his boss. General Whitehead's eyes told him that he should sit down and shut up. He settled in his seat.

The FBI Director spoke about al-Qaeda's plan to establish headquarters in Newark, and eventually set off simultaneous attacks of biological weapons in five American cities.

Taylor felt his checks flush. He wanted to scream at the Joint Chiefs: *What's the problem? Just exterminate the bastards in their camps.*

The FBI Director reported on more bad news: A few al-Qaeda had entered the US and had attempted to release anthrax in an office building in New York City, but they were captured before releasing it. He agreed with General Taylor that the terrorists failed in '93, but they were definitely coming back.

Taylor rose. He couldn't hold back his rage. "I think it's time to take immediate action. If we wait, hundreds of Middle Easterners will slip through." The FBI Director nodded in agreement.

"And what do you suggest we do, General Taylor?" said Chairman Meacham.

Taylor answered, "Stop them from entering this country."

"How?" said the admiral, inhaling with a couple of snorts.

"The INS. They're the problem. They allow terrorists to flood into our country."

"What do you mean?" said the Chief of the Air Force, sitting straight in his chair, appearing the most concerned.

Taylor explained that in a recent *60 Minutes* report on the INS, dozens of Middle Easterners were shown entering this country as they get off planes in New York City. INS wasn't sending them back. All that the immigrants had to say to the INS agents was the magic word: "asylum." They were then told to report back on a certain day, but most never did. Also, there were thousands in this country on visas. No one knew where they were.

"The FBI knows this," said Taylor. Everyone turned in unison to look for a response from the Director.

The Director nodded. "That's correct."

"I'm sure that's being changed," said the Air Force Chief.

"Not true," said Taylor. "If it were, why is the FBI Director here? He just said there's a buildup in New Jersey. How did they get here? There's only one answer to that—"

The FBI Director interrupted him. "I'm afraid General Taylor's right, gentlemen. We've asked the President and Congress numerous times to change some of the immigration laws. So far nothing. We interrupt this to mean no one wants to touch the immigration problem for fear of raising the do-gooder giant."

Silence fell upon the room, while the Chiefs looked at each other. No one had the courage to add to, or criticize, what the Director had said. Taylor knew the chiefs would never take a stand, so it was up to him.

The chairman leaned in toward the directors, speaking in a whisper. There was mumbling from others in the room. The admiral turned to the group and said, "I believe we need to look into this more. We'll talk with the Secretary and meet again on this. That's all for now," he said as he rose from his chair.

General Taylor jumped up by his chair. "Admiral Meacham? Sir?" Meacham scowled at Taylor.

"We can't wait, sir. The President and Secretary Lewis must think about bombing al-Qaeda training camps now. This can't wait. Those in our cities must be rounded up before we suffer tremendous losses."

The chairman's face hardened. "General Taylor, I've indicated we'll take this up later."

———— • ————

Standing at the back of the room with Taylor, General Whitehead saw Meacham motioning for him to come forward. He waited until the others had left before moving to the front.

"Yes, Admiral," said Whitehead. He knew the chairman was pissed.

"I'm detecting antagonism in General Taylor's behavior, Allen. Is he going to be a problem, again?" They walked to the door and strode through the corridor.

"You know how he is when it comes to terrorism," said Whitehead. "He'll be okay."

This was the Chairman's way of telling him to keep Taylor in check, and not to embarrass the Pentagon again. This wasn't the first time Whitehead had had to come to Taylor's defense. Project Game Point's failure had tarnished the Army's image in the Pentagon, exposing the DoD's secret testing program—using agents on civilians and military personnel. All the military branches did it. Only Taylor got caught at it.

"I'll talk to him," said Whitehead.

"See that you do," said Meacham. "Don't want him embarrassing us again. Need I remind you? Senator Fellows is waiting for us to screw up."

"I understand, sir. I'll see to it that Taylor stays in line."

———— ◆ ————

General Taylor returned to his Pentagon office, eased into his leather chair, clasped his hands behind his head, and smiled. Exposing his feelings about the terrorists the way he did raised his spirits. Someone had to tell the Joint Chiefs the truth. Taylor knew Whitehead would call him in and chew on his ass for challenging the Chairman.

Whitehead's a weakling, and so is Meacham. They just don't get it. It's up to me.

He reached for the phone and called Mors.

"How can I help you, Princeton?"

"The FBI's captured al-Qaeda documents that confirm the DIA's findings." He paused to calm himself. "Al-Qaeda is planning to move into New Jersey to train militants to form cells in other American cities."

Before Mors could say anything more, Taylor said, "If my bioweapon were ready, I'd wipe out all the Middle East training camps."

"That's what I like to hear, Princeton," said Mors.

"APAT can get 'em here, and I'll get 'em over there."

"That's the spirit," said Mors. "Once you identify the cells here, APAT will execute them."

CHAPTER THIRTY-ONE

They never saw their leader, knew him only as Mors, a coded name. He only spoke to them through the "Box"—a special telephone hookup.

Two-dozen members had gathered in a hideaway building in the woods outside DC. Security was tight, and IDs were checked.

Mors had called this special meeting.

He had been giving them the latest intelligence information, and the bright afternoon sun did little to raise their spirits.

The Defense Intelligence Agency had known for some time that Middle East terrorists were engaged in experiments dealing with anthrax and typhus. But now the DIA had hard evidence that the terrorists had begun production of other pathogens.

APAT, an eclectic group of individuals high in government, the military and corporations, was unhappy with the way Washington bureaucrats had handled Homeland Security. It was virtually nonexistent. APAT's mission was to assume responsibility for Homeland Security by executing terrorists.

"More bad news," said Mors. "Intelligence has captured computers and e-mails that reveal a plan to establish terrorist cells in this country for the purpose of releasing biologicals in our cities."

"Which group?" asked a Navy commander.

"Al-Qaeda," said Mors.

"Do we know which cities?" asked an Army Colonel.

"No," said Mors. "Not yet."

"When al-Qaeda enters this country, let's hit 'em with all we got," said one CEO.

A retired FBI agent stood up, faced the group, and said, "It's better to wait until the first cell is fully established in one of our cities before we make our move."

"That's right," said Mors. "That will stop the cancer from growing. Capture and execute. That's our mantra."

"We'll show the arrogant bastards in Congress how Homeland Security should work," said a businessman. "Their bickering has put our country in grave danger."

"What about the FBI?" asked a government official. "They may be on to us."

"For the moment, they're too busy trying to outsmart the other intelligence agencies to worry about our movements," said the retired FBI agent. "They couldn't track a bleeding elephant in the snow."

Laughter.

"Have the weapons been distributed?" asked Mors.

"Yes," said the Army Colonel. "We've already had two practices in the field."

"Good," said Mors. "Stand ready."

CHAPTER THIRTY-TWO

When Matt Brenner pulled into the parking lot at DnaTech Pharmaceuticals, he saw a military chopper parked on the pad behind the main office building. *The general's here. I'll have to be careful.* He had told Special Agent Chris Cousins this was the night he'd break into Taylor's office.

Around noon, Matt left his lab and turned into the corridor that dead-ended at Taylor's office and the conference room. If the general's door were open, he'd wait and go later. He approached, and saw the door was closed. He glanced at the ceiling camera at the far corner, noticing that it didn't scan the area in front of Taylor's office.

Lucky for me, he thought. Who needs to watch the general anyway?

Matt eased closer to the door. He could hear Taylor talking on the phone. "Mors," was mentioned. Then Taylor's voice got louder. "St. Louis virus," he said, plain as day and, "it mutates."

Footsteps. Adrenaline ripped through Matt's veins. He dashed into the corner and pressed his back up against the wall, holding his breath. A man in green scrubs strode through the side corridor and never looked Matt's way.

Matt exhaled and rushed to his office. He felt a high from the endorphins circulating in his body as he thought about the mystery that hung over Mors. The FBI suspected that the APAT leader was someone high in government. According to Chris, Mors had recruited Taylor for APAT because of his ultra-conservative politics, and his outspoken condemnation of terrorists after the 1993 bombing of the World Trade Center.

———— ◆ ————

Thirty minutes after midnight, Matt left his office clothed in black: a ski mask, fleece wear and gloves. The corridor lights had been dimmed for the evening, and he inched along the wall like a cat burglar. He stood for a minute in front of Taylor's office, then pushed his credit card in between the lock and the doorjamb, emulating what he had seen in the movies. The lock clicked. He pushed on the door, inching it open. He twisted his six-inch Maglite flashlight on and scanned the office, looking for a camera. None. He moved in and closed the door.

The small office had a desk and a side-arm chair that Taylor had probably taken from the conference room. Nothing was on the walls, or on the desk or on the bookshelves. Two green four-drawer filing cabinets stood in the corner behind the desk like two soldiers at attention. The air smelled stale, and after removing the ski mask he felt a waft of air on his face. He moved to the filing cabinets and pulled several homemade keys made out of fingernail files from his belt.

The key shook in his hand as he inserted it into the lock at the top of the first filing cabinet. It didn't work. After trying a third key, the lock popped out. He reached for the drawer handle, but stopped. *What if it's rigged with a silent alarm? Ash and his men will be on me.*

Matt held his breath while he inched out the drawer until it stopped, shoved it in, and hurried out, closing the door after him. He darted across the hall and slipped into the conference room. Standing behind the door, he listened for footsteps. Twenty minutes later, he decided the drawer hadn't been rigged. He went back into Taylor's office and opened the drawer again.

He thumbed through four drawers. *Where are "APAT" and "Entropy"?*

He picked the lock on the next cabinet. "Great God," he murmured to himself, "here they are in plain sight." He pulled the files out, threw them on Taylor's desk, and slammed the drawer shut with his elbow. He replaced his ski mask, picked up the documents, and eased out of the office.

After he finished copying the documents, Matt locked them in his desk, edged his way through the corridor, then stopped.

Instantly alert, alarmed by what he saw. It took a few seconds for him to register what he was looking at.

Two men with mops and buckets stood in the middle of the hallway talking. Against the wall were buffing machines. *They're going to strip and rewax the floor. That'll take hours.*

Matt slipped back around the corner. The custodians were taking their sweet time of it and will probably take breaks before the night was over. He returned to his office, flopped in his chair. The digital desk clock showed 2:30. He rubbed a hand through his hair.

When he had checked on Taylor's movements during his monthly visits to the Center, Matt learned that the general arrived at his office at six every morning without fail. *The son of a bitch loves discipline.*

The custodians were stripping the wax from the floor at three-thirty, not appearing in any hurry.

At four-thirty, he returned to the corridor and found the workers mopping the floor.

"Chrissake! They haven't starting waxing yet. I'll never get the documents back in time." He inhaled a deep breath. *Got to stay calm.*

Matt returned to the corridor at five-thirty, this time carrying the documents and dressed in his street clothes. He had thirty minutes before General Taylor came to his office. *It's now or never.* The workers were out of sight. *Have they finished, or were they on break?* The buffer machines were further down the corridor past the short hallway to Taylor's office. Matt crept through the corridor, watching for the two men. He approached the corner, and he peered around the edge. No one.

He slipped into Taylor's office, replaced the documents, and eased back into the hall. He turned the corner, then he stopped. His heart raced.

General Taylor was at the far end of the corridor arguing with someone. They were in each other's face, and they hadn't seen Matt. Maybe Taylor'll think I'm just coming to work, he thought. But everyone knows I never get here this early.

Matt moved along the wall, praying that Taylor wouldn't turn and look his way. Seconds seemed like minutes as he inched his way toward his office, about thirty yards from where the general was standing. Matt thought about running, but any swift movement could catch the general's eye. He finally made it, collapsed in his chair, and sighed. *That was too close.*

He opened the desk drawer, smiled and pulled out the documents, and read them. Forty-five minutes later, he rose, threw the documents into his briefcase, and went to the elevator. Taylor had gone.

As he waited for the corporal to wave him through the gate, Matt pulled the FBI cell phone from his pocket and left Chris a message: "Posh Nosh at two o'clock."

CHAPTER THIRTY-THREE

That early afternoon a cool breeze had developed, and Matt's spirits were high. *We're getting closer to Jack's killers.*

The Posh Nosh deli was on the north side of Clayton, a few miles from his townhouse. On the way, he kept an eye on the rearview mirror. He pulled into the back of the building, grabbed his briefcase, and alighted from the BMW. He hurried to the front entrance, entered a little before two o'clock, and regarded the place. The room was long and narrow with cream-colored walls, hung with a few pictures of deli food and lighting fixtures reminiscent of the oil-lamp era.

He made his way between ice cream parlor tables and chairs. Circulating ceiling fans were arranged in a straight line that led to the back. Square cardboard signs with pictures of Budweiser beer and corn beef sandwiches dangled below them.

Two college students sat at a table hugging and kissing. Books and loose-leaf notebooks with Washington University logos were unopened on the table, but studying was far from their minds. Orders were placed at a counter to his left. Farther down, separated by a large glass refrigerator case with an assortment of meats and cheeses, was another counter where orders were picked up. The smell of sour pickles hung in the air. A coed dressed in a Washington University T-shirt stood behind the counter, glaring at Matt.

"A cup of coffee, black," he said.

Chris sat in the back under the exit sign, waving at him. Matt went to the table and greeted him with a nod, set his coffee and briefcase on the table, and took the seat next to him, facing the front. Two large windows on each side of the entrance gave them a good view of the street. He could see the passing cars. A perfect spot, he thought. They could dart out the back if they had to.

"Anyone follow you?"

"Didn't see anyone."

"Good. Let's have them."

Matt flipped the latches on his briefcase, pulled out the files, and handed them to the FBI agent, who grabbed them like a child eager for a treat. Glancing over them, Chris shook his head and whispered, "This is great stuff."

Matt sipped his coffee.

"I presume you've read these," said Chris as he closed the last file.

"What do you think?" said Matt.

Chris smiled. "You're really enjoying this, aren't you?"

Matt blinked hard at him. "I think so."

The APAT document was an organizational chart with a listing of the membership by name and titles. APAT consisted of government officials, scientists, military officers, and CEOs of giant corporations. Nothing in the document identified Mors or Taylor. Mors had the title Commander-in-Chief, and the General of the Army had to be Taylor.

ENTROPY, written by General Taylor in 1996, three years after the World Trade Center bombing, was APAT's strategic plan for attacking terrorists in American cities. General Taylor's role as commanding officer over antiterrorist operations was illuminated in the organizational chart. By virtue of his position within the Intelligence Community of the Pentagon, General Taylor would know firsthand when terrorists entered American cities. Mors would decide when and where APAT would attack like a militia. Matt leaned in to the table. "Since Taylor's privy to all classified information, how can you stop him? He knows when things happen before they happen."

Chris looked past Matt, sipping his coffee. Then he turned and locked on Matt's gaze. "Trust me. We'll know."

CHAPTER THIRTY-FOUR

Matt dressed for his run, left the townhouse around six, and dashed through the streets filled with excitement over his discovery of a designer enzyme. At the end of his run, he decided against coffee and a bagel at Rosens' Deli and raced home. This morning, they would test the enzyme in mice.

His research group had recombined genes in hundreds of different ways until they created this new entity with thirty-two genes—each sliced from a different bacterium, resulting in the production of a powerful enzyme. *In vitro* testing using Petri dishes and culture flasks had demonstrated that the designer enzyme had dissolved all the pathogens used in the experiments. Matt hypothesized that his GSE protein, or Gene Shuffling Enzyme protein, could be used as an antidote, dissolving lethal bacteria and viruses. He smiled, thinking that his colleagues in the scientific community would ridicule his discovery and call him crazy, because no one had gone this far in gene shuffling.

He entered his townhouse, showered and dressed. Before leaving for DnaTech, he went into his home office and called Mark Devlin, the *Post-Dispatch* reporter. He had called him several times in the past week and left messages, but Devlin never returned his calls

---

"I'm going to need your help in the Level 4, Joan," said Matt into his cell phone, driving to DnaTech.

"On the GSE?" she said.

"Yes, I'll send over my report on the *in vitro* studies we did. I'm excited about the results." He slowed at a yellow traffic signal.

"I'm eager to read your report," said Joan.

"Today we're infecting the HIS-mice with the IL-4 mousepox virus and treating with the GSE. If the protein works, I'd like for you to test it against one of your biologicals in the monkey. Could you do that for us?"

"I have just the agent, ME-347, but I should clear it with Don."

"Is that necessary? I thought you were in charge of the maximum containment labs."

"I am, but I'll be using monkeys. He'll have to approve the protocol."

"Is there any way you can hold off telling him? I don't want to show my hand. Don't know what Taylor'll do if he knows we had an antidote."

"Let me handle it," she said.

"I'm heading to the office," he said, snapping the cell phone shut.

Peter was in the animal room talking with Melissa when Matt entered. Ginger stood at one of the cages examining the HIS-mice. Peter turned and when he saw Matt, he said, "The infected HIS-mice are ready, Boss."

"Which cage contains the control group?" That group was infected, but wouldn't receive the GSE protein.

"It's this one," Ginger said, slapping the cage nearest Matt. She then moved a hand over the top of two cages, and said, "These two contain twenty-four mice each and will be treated with GSE."

"Good," said Matt. "Let's get with it. Who has the GSE vials?"

"I do," said Peter, holding up a plastic stand containing many vials filled with a straw-colored liquid. "Melissa took them out of the freezer this morning." He handed the stand to her.

Matt slipped on rubber gloves. "Peter, you take the first cage, and I'll take the second."

Peter nodded. Melissa and Ginger stood behind the two men filling syringes with the antidote. Melissa handed the first syringe to Peter, and Ginger handed another to Matt.

Two hours later, Peter said, "That's the last one, Boss."

"One more and I'll be done," said Matt.

Moments later, Matt closed the cage door and locked it. "That's it for me," he said. He looked at the wall clock. "Let's go to lunch."

"When will we know if the GSE worked, Dr. Brenner?" asked Melissa.

"Just keep an eye on the control group," he said. "Then we'll know."

———— ◆ ————

Later that evening, Matt drove into his driveway and noticed he had forgotten to throw his newspaper on the stoop this morning. He parked, left the BMW without closing the door, and went to the curb to retrieve it. He placed the paper under his arm, went to the BMW, removed his briefcase, and slammed the door.

In his kitchen, he threw the car keys on the breakfast bar, dropped his briefcase on the counter, went to the overstuffed chair, and opened the newspaper.

"Oh, no," he moaned.

In large print: *POST-DISPATCH REPORTER DROWNED IN A BOATING ACCIDENT.* The story under Devlin's picture explained that Mark's body had washed to shore the day before, about five miles south of St. Louis. The current had taken his boat several miles farther downstream. The medical examiner had determined that Devlin had been dead over a week.

Matt dropped the paper to the floor and stared at the wall.

It was no accident. Someone killed him.

The FBI cell phone went off, playing a musical tune he didn't recognize. *It has to be Chris.* Matt went to his briefcase to retrieve it.

"Chris?"

"Have you read the paper?"

"Just now."

"Our van picked up some unusual messages between a deputy and the Police Chief."

"What was it?"

"Can't tell you."

"Why are you guys listening in on the police station?"

"We're on to someone."

CHAPTER THIRTY-FIVE

Matt had confided in Peter about Devlin connecting the mayor and police chief with someone in the Biodefense Center. Probably the general.

"Boss, you know his death was no accident."

"Mark was on to someone, Peter. I wish I knew who."

"It's the same old story," said Peter. "When you stick your nose in where it doesn't belong, bad things happen."

Matt stared at Peter, thinking he'd heard that bullshit before. *It's what people say when they're afraid to take on the big boys.*

"Hey, I've got some good news for you," said Peter. "Let's go to the animal room."

Melissa and Ginger stood by the cage with the control group, wearing huge smiles on their faces. He moved closer when the techs opened the cage door and moved aside.

"They're all dead," said Peter.

Melissa and Ginger opened the doors of the other two cages, and Peter moved in front of them and said, "Look at these."

"Great God! They're all alive!" shouted Matt.

After their excitement had subsided, Matt told the group that to determine if the antidote was effective, they'd have to watch the animals for seventy-two hours.

CHAPTER THIRTY-SIX

In the Hawaiian Club, Matt saw Colonel Jagger sitting alone at a table against the wall in the dining area. He dodged waiters bustling between tables, serving the lunch crowd. Matt wondered what Jagger wanted.

"Have a seat, Dr. Brenner," said Jagger, gesturing.

Matt pulled the chair from the table and sat. He looked at Jagger's once-broken nose, but didn't know why his eyes went there every time they met. What was this fascination he had with it? He just did, that's all.

The waiter arrived with menus. Jagger ordered a turkey sandwich with Swiss cheese, and Brenner chose the Caesar salad.

Jagger reached for his water and placed it by his plate. "The general's been pressuring me about your antibiological. How's it going?"

Matt's eyes narrowed. He took a few seconds before answering. "Is there anything particular the general would like to know?"

"When you'll be testing it."

Matt's muscles tightened. He watched Jagger as he sipped his water and placed it on the table.

"I have to be honest," said Jagger. "The general's the type that has to see before he believes."

Faithless heretic, Matt thought.

He waited until the waiter had placed the salad in front of him before saying, "Had a little setback—"

Jagger interrupted. "I'm afraid the general'll be pissed about a setback. Can you give me anything encouraging to tell him?"

Yeah. Tell him to go fuck himself. Matt disliked anyone looking over his shoulder.

"Had to switch to DNA shuffling. As it turns out, that was a good thing. The antidote we're preparing now will do a better job destroying both bacteria and viruses."

"Well, that's good news. He'll be pleased to hear that."

"Should I prepare a report?" said Matt, not that he wanted to, but thought that might appease the colonel.

"Only if he asks me for it. He'll want you to test it as soon as possible. Can I tell him when that'll be?" Jagger took a bite of his sandwich.

"In a few weeks," said Matt, pausing at the thought about saying what was on his mind. "Colonel, I'm troubled over another matter."

"And what might that be?"

"A silver Buick sedan has been following me for weeks. Know anything about it?"

Jagger frowned. "No."

"It has to be military. I want them off my ass."

"I should say. Let me check into it."

Back in his office, Jagger reached for the red phone. He had decided he wouldn't tell Taylor about the setback.

"General? Brenner's testing his antidote in a few weeks. Says it'll be very effective against both bacteria and viruses."

"He's bullshitting us to stall for time."

"Don't think so. He's been working hard."

"Brenner's an independent cuss," said the general. "Keep the heat on him. We need that antidote."

"Sir, Brenner's upset that a silver Buick sedan has been following him for some time. Is that DIA?"

"Son of a bitch," said Taylor. "It's Ash."

"Brenner's pissed about it. I'm concerned he'll slow his work if it doesn't stop."

"Ash's paranoid. Thinks all civilians are against us. I'll take care of it."

CHAPTER THIRTY-SEVEN

She stood next to the big man and said, "It's been a long time since I've been down here in the Surveillance Center, Don. I see your people are still at it."

He nodded, turned, and went to his desk.

Joan followed him and settled in the only chair facing him.

"Now, what is it you wanted to see me about?" asked she.

"It's about ME-347," he said.

"The slatewiper? It's some scary bug." She paused. "As you know, it wiped out all the animals we infected, turning them to mush."

She noticed that Jagger hadn't been paying attention to her, so she stopped and said, "What's up, Don? You seem miles away."

"It's about ME-347."

"What about it?"

"It's ours," he said.

"Ours?" She squirmed in her seat. "What do you mean—ours?"

"ME-347 is the coded name the general made up. It's a hybrid virus."

He explained how Max developed it by eliminating the gene responsible for causing polio. The modified poliovirus still invaded motor neurons in the brain, but didn't cause polio. Then, Max allowed the Game Point virus to exchange some of its DNA with the modified poliovirus, giving rise to the hybrid that the general named ME-347.

"Max expected his hybrid to enter the brain and destroy the entire nervous system," said the colonel.

"Why did Max lie to me?"

"The general told him to. To keep you from challenging the

general's work."

She jumped up and paced the room to shake off her disbelief. Then she said, "Yeah. He knew I'd squawk."

"I'm afraid so."

She stopped in front of his desk and glared at him.

"If anyone in Congress ever found out about this, they'd crucify us."

In the mid-1980s, the USAMRIID had changed its research direction from biologicals to biodefense because of Congress. When the Biodefense Center at DnaTech had been conceived in the mid-1990s, the plan included only germ defense, and DnaTech was willing to manufacture all the vaccines the Army wanted. Other pharmaceutical companies had bailed out, afraid of lawsuits and profit loss if their vaccines weren't used. The Army guaranteed DnaTech a reasonable profit. It only took months to develop an offensive weapon-grade agent, but years to develop a vaccine against it. Many in the Army were unhappy with the new direction, particularly General Taylor.

Jagger raised a hand. "Joan. Stop a minute and think about the new enemy. He wears no uniform and he'd not hesitate for a second to release some nasty shit on us."

She knew he was right, but didn't like being involved in a conspiracy to deceive Whitehead. He was the stalwart that had pushed hard for defensive measures to protect this country. She'd like to report this to him, but she knew better. The military didn't like whistleblowers. Oh, they'd put on a good show for the media, but then they'd make her life miserable, maybe threaten court-martial, but certainly assign her to shit details.

"What about General Whitehead?" she asked, flopping into her chair.

Jagger rubbed his face with a big hand. "I know where you're going with this," he said. "If you'd rather not get involved, we can get Major Kozlowski to continue the work."

He's not answering my question. I shouldn't have mentioned Whitehead.

"I trained Derek in the Blue suit," she said. "He's very good."

The colonel moved forward in his chair. "Well, I guess we're through here."

Joan didn't like the idea of Derek taking over her lab, and Jagger knew it. *He's playing on my emotions,* she thought. Call it territorial, but she had built the maximum containment lab and was in charge since it opened. Morally, she didn't like going against the Army Chief of Staff, nor did she like defrauding the government, but she couldn't stand having Derek take over the Hot Zone. They may even transfer her. *Shit,* she thought, *they have me over a barrel.*

"Why does the general want this biological? Be up front with me."

"From the beginning, the general never agreed with Congress or the military on destroying all biologicals and abandoning all biological research. He felt by doing so, it gave the terrorists an advantage. The same advantage as if we had destroyed all our nuclear capability, and yet allowed the Russians to keep theirs."

"You mean fight fire with fire?" she added.

He smiled. "Something like that."

"What if we're found out? What then?"

"The buck stops at the general's doorstep. He commands this place. He's the one giving the order to proceed with the testing."

Joan sighed. "It's a perversion of science to develop biologicals, and maybe it's even a perversion to work on defensive measures when you stop to think about it." She paused, making sure what she said next would be printed indelibly on his brain. "I'll do it; however, I want it noted for the record that I'm not in agreement, nor am I comfortable working on offensive weapons."

"That's fine," said Jagger. He moved forward in his chair.

"There's something else."

He described how Max put the St. Louis virus in the well of a computer chip and how it could be stimulated.

"The computer as a bioweapon?" she said.

"That's what makes it so unique."

Joan didn't like Jagger's excitement over the new bioweapon.

"Max is calling the mutant Omega Bytes."

"When do you want to test the chip?"

"I'll have Max contact you," said Jagger.

She rose and went to the door, then stopped when she remembered Matt's antidote.

"Oh, I nearly forgot. Matt Brenner's working on an antidote that should please you."

"He told me about it over lunch."

Joan frowned. "Did he tell you it's a protein enzyme that could dissolve both bacteria and viruses?"

The colonel's eyebrows rose. "You mean like those enzymes in soap powder that eat stains off clothing?"

"That's a little elementary, but it's close enough."

Jagger's large face expanded with a smile. "Test it against Omega Bytes."

"It's not quite ready."

She made sure she didn't betray Matt's confidence by telling Jagger it was ready. If word got back to the general, it could mean the end of both of them. She remembered what Dostoyevsky had said, something to the effect: Nothing was easier than to denounce the evil one, yet nothing was more difficult than to understand him.

CHAPTER THIRTY-EIGHT

Driving to work the next morning, Joan braked behind a red Camaro, idling at a traffic light. She began rubbing her hands around the steering wheel and squirmed in her seat. When the Camaro didn't lunge forward the instant the light changed, Joan honked her horn several times and shouted, "What are you waiting for?" The woman flipped her the finger and raced off. Joan took a deep breath and exhaled as she drove through the intersection. *I need to calm down. Can't let them get to me.*

Her meeting with Jagger made her mad as hell. She didn't like being lied to. Worst of all, she allowed herself to be sucked into the general's bioweapon research.

Joan pulled into her parking space. Knowing what she had to do, she climbed out of the car and dashed into the building, rode the red elevator to the sixth floor, and hurried to Matt's lab. She found him at the island bench talking with Peter Crane, motioned for him to follow her into his office, closed the door behind her, and stood by the chair.

"I'm pissed."

"I can see that. What'd I do?"

"Nothing."

Matt moved forward in his chair. "Why don't you take a seat and tell me what's got you so worked up?"

She complied. "I've got some bad news." She paused.

"Yes, yes. What is it?"

"Max and the general... they've developed a superbug from Game Point. Max called me last night. He's afraid the general's going to release it in this country."

Scientists feared the day a microbe could be manipulated into a bug with super powers: one that had no incubation period, traveled

112

like a juggernaut, and killed ninety percent of everything in its path. A slatewiper.

"Are you sure it's a slatewiper?"

"Hell yes. I tested the damn thing. Turned the animals into mush."

Mush means no incubation period. Most pathogens required an incubation period of days or weeks to amplify in the host's cells before symptoms appeared. No incubation period meant immediate death.

"Max lied to me to get it tested," said Joan, when Matt turned back and looked at her. "Told me DIA captured a biological in the Middle East, coded ME-347."

Joan described how Max had developed his microchip and weaponized the virus using the computer as its delivery system.

"He's named his mutant Omega Bytes," she said. "I know what you're thinking. I didn't question his motives because our goal has always been to find antidotes or vaccines for the terrorists' biologicals."

Matt rose and came from behind his desk. "Taylor had this planned all along. Probably thought of developing a biological even before the Center was finished." He paused. "The bastard's smart. He's used Peter's work on vaccines to camouflage this place. To dupe the top brass into thinking he had established a true Biodefense Center."

"What are we going to do? We're testing the microchip the day after tomorrow."

Matt returned to his seat, but when he didn't respond, she fell silent.

"Contact General Whitehead," said Matt.

"I thought of that, but dismissed it. Remember that wall of secrecy?"

"But I'm a civilian. He'd believe me."

"So was Jack Sinclair."

"What about some politician?" he asked.

"Not a good idea," she said. "Many are in bed with the military."

"Then there's only one thing left for us—"

She interrupted him. "What's that?"

"You must test my GSE protein."

"Can do."

"Did you tell Jagger about it?"

"He loved it. Ordered me to test it against Omega Bytes."

He frowned. "You didn't tell him it was ready?"

"No way. Word would get back to the general."

"I'll get some vials to you."

"What if the antidote doesn't work in humans?" she said.

"It will."

"Can you mass-produce it?" she asked.

"DnaTech will mass-produce it. I have about fifty doses."

"What if Taylor releases Omega Bytes before we have enough antidote?"

"Then we're doomed," said Matt. "And so are millions of innocent people."

CHAPTER THIRTY-NINE

Seated at a computer in the Surveillance Tracking Center next to Colonel Jagger, Max Tandenbaum looked up at the huge wall screen displaying a clear view of the Level 4 laboratory.

Behind him stood General Taylor and Captain Ash, and off to the side were a few white coats invited by Taylor. All were focused on Major Joan Wu and Sergeant Marlowe in the maximum containment laboratory moving about in space suits preparing for today's test of the Omega Bytes microchip. Max looked at his watch.

"One-thirty," said Max. "It's time." Turning to General Taylor, "We won't see anything for about sixty minutes after I send in the coded message."

"You're in charge," said Taylor, lowering himself into a seat on Max's left. "Begin when you're ready."

Marlowe stood by a rabbit cage at the opposite end of the room, while Joan watched the cage on the bench a few feet away from the Omega Bytes computer.

"Ready in Level 4?" Max asked.

"Ready," said Joan.

Max's fingers tapped the keys, sending the command to the programmed electronics board in the computer stationed in the lab.

Fifty minutes had passed and he turned to the general, who was looking at his watch. No one moved. Muscles tightened. Eyes fixed on the wide screen. Stillness like that in outer space overtook the room.

"Sixty minutes," shouted Taylor.

Nothing.

Max growled, "What's wrong, Major?"

"Nothing that I can see."

"Check your commands, Dr. Tandenbaum," said Taylor.

Max rolled his eyes, jumped to his feet, and bumped his legs against his chair on rollers, sailing it behind him.

"Sergeant? Check the damn computer board in Omega Bytes," said Max. Like walking on the moon, Marlowe ambled over to the computer, removed the top, and examined the interior.

"Here's the problem. The chip's not snapped into place." He replaced the top, and then gave Joan the thumbs-up.

"We're ready," said Joan.

Max began tapping the keys. Everyone watched for the drama to begin. Taylor mentioned that thirty minutes had elapsed. The room was still.

After sixty minutes, the rabbits in the metal cages became agitated.

The cameras zoomed in on the cages. Three rabbits in the cage close to Marlowe circled in frenzy. They began attacking one another. One jumped on the thick, wire-meshed door, hanging by its claws, attempting to chew its way out. Another fell over on its side. Seconds later, all rabbits fell on their backs, legs jerking in rapid kicks. Watchers in the Surveillance Center jumped up, holding their breaths.

"Son of a bitch," someone shouted. "Look at that."

Liquid oozed from one of the animals, then another, and another.

"They're dissolving," another shouted.

Silence fell on the room.

Joan said, "They're all dead. Nothing but fur and bones in a sticky liquid."

Taylor, on his feet, turned to Jagger. "We have our bioweapon."

Max saw the door close as Ash left the room, and wondered where he was going. He turned to the large screen. *It's like the rabbits slid out of their fur.*

"Dr. Tandenbaum," said Taylor, slapping him on the back, "you've done it, you've done it. Congratulations!"

Max didn't respond. He was busy watching Marlowe. Jagger whispered to Max, "Sergeant Marlowe's acting strange."

Everyone in the room was on his feet.

"Major? Check the sergeant," said Max. *He's probably done something stupid again.*

Marlowe lurched, pulled on his air hose, yanking it off. He reached for another one, but before he could attach it, he fell against the bench. Joan shuffled over to him.

"What's wrong?" she shouted at him. He pointed to his air hose. Anguish flooded his blanched face. He gasped for air like a fish out of water. She tried to connect the hose, but he pushed her away. She shoved him toward the large metal door, but inches from it, he fell to his knees, hitting his head on the door. His helmet flew off. She grabbed it and pulled it down over his face.

"Oh my God," shouted Joan. "Max, we've got to get Sergeant Marlowe into the Slammer."

She pushed Marlowe against the wall next to the airlock steel door and unlatched it. The door flew open, and she shoved him into the decon-shower room. It took all her energy to hold him up against the shower wall with her body. Then she engaged the shower, allowing disinfectant to flow over both of them. While she waited, Joan realized that if it weren't for her aerobics class and the weight-strengthening exercises she couldn't have held Marlowe up in the space suit.

When the shower stopped, Joan dragged Marlowe's body into the staging area holding his arm around her neck and placing her other arm around his waist. Two soldiers in space suits met them and carried Marlowe away. Witnesses in the Surveillance Center froze. Max darted out of the room.

"What happened in there?" said Max, as he met Joan, who hadn't changed out of her Blue suit, and was about to enter the hospital suite for Level 4 accidents.

"Something happened to his air hose. I've got to go in."

The suite was under negative pressure and enclosed by double steel doors. She watched the Army nurse open the tent that circled the bio-isolation bed in anticipation of Marlowe's arrival. The soldiers laid his naked body on the bed. The nurse and doctor, wearing space suits, attended to the sergeant. Joan stood at the foot of the bed, staring at the unconscious body.

"He's burning up," said the nurse.

The doctor nodded. "His skin is turning scarlet and blotchy."

Marlowe coughed and blood gushed from his mouth. The blotches had turned into patches resembling smallpox that grew wider and leaked blood.

Joan thought how Marlowe had supported her when Richard had died. She was at a loss to help him.

Marlowe convulsed. The doctor looked at the nurse and said, "He's crashing and bleeding out."

Marlowe's skin began separating from his body and liquid oozed.

"Oh my God," said Joan. "His cells are exploding."

She stared at his face. *I'm so sorry, Sergeant.*

Convoluted folds formed on his face and body. His face disappeared as the skin slid down over his chin, exposing a skull with sunken sockets. Bony fingertips pointed at Joan. Gooey liquid like lava dripped off the sheet, forming puddles on the floor. All that remained of Sergeant Fred Marlowe was hair and a skeleton embedded in a gelatinous mass.

CHAPTER FORTY

Back in the Surveillance Center, General Taylor looked over the group of stunned researchers. Max had returned and reported on the death of Sergeant Marlowe and how the virus had dissolved his body.

General Taylor became ecstatic when he heard how Omega Bytes had devoured Sergeant Marlowe. He now had a biological that no country could connect to the US military. He felt his acting—faking his shock—wasn't all that bad. The intense stimulation from knowing that his bioweapon was ready and wouldn't be tested in the field almost gave him an orgasm.

"There's not much else we can do," he said to Jagger as he rose, and turned to the group of white coats standing around the room in shock.

"Let me have your attention, everyone. I know we've witnessed a tragic event, and our hearts and prayers go out to Sergeant Marlowe's family, but we must get back to work. I'll keep you informed as we gather the facts. Dismissed."

The researchers filed out of the room. Taylor waited. Captain Ash entered and winked at the general.

"Let's meet in the conference room," said Taylor to Jagger and Ash as he led the way. Taylor went to the front, and Jagger and Ash sat at the conference table.

"Gentlemen, what we don't want is a leak to the press. Agreed?"
They nodded.

The door opened. Heads turned. Max entered and took a seat.
"Will there be a report?" said Ash.
"You'll see to it," said Taylor.
"Captain Ash has all the details about Sergeant Marlowe. I think

he's the best person." Turning to him, Taylor said, "You take care of it, Brian."

Max raised a hand.

Taylor ignored him and said, "The report will show Sergeant Marlowe's death a suicide. We know that the sergeant had been visiting a psychiatrist at Barnes for his depression. Anything to add, Captain Ash?"

"Yes, sir, General," he said, standing. "I took Sergeant Marlowe to Barnes on several visits to his psychiatrist, which are documented. Also, on several occasions I saved him from taking his life."

Max stood, staring at Taylor.

"I see this as an accident," said Max, "and it should be ruled as one until there is a complete investigation." He paused. "It's definitely no suicide."

Taylor glowered. *You ungrateful drunk. I saved your ass from the pit, and now you're turning on me.*

Jagger glared at Max. "We do have evidence of Marlowe's mental instability."

The general snorted. "We do. It's all documented. Sergeant Marlowe had mental problems and that's what the investigation will show." He turned away from Max's stare and looked at the two officers. "Keep these facts under wraps until I release the report on the cause of death."

CHAPTER FORTY-ONE

Major Derek Zolowsky entered the red elevator that whisked him up to the sixth floor. His small office was located in the microbiology department and, like the other offices, had no windows. That didn't concern him since he spent little time there. He loved the lab.

Zolowsky earned his Ph.D. in genetics and microbiology from Washington University and had become an expert in electron microscopy. The mysterious nature of the Hot Zone microbes had fired his passion for understanding their genetic makeup.

He went to the lunchroom to get a cup of coffee, then returned to his office, leaned back in his chair, and placed his feet on the desk. He thought about how Joan Wu had approached him about assisting her in testing Brenner's antidote in the monkey. She felt she had to tell him about the background on the Omega Bytes virus. He remembered that his reaction had surprised her. He told her he could care less and didn't engage in Center politics. Research was all he cared about, and he left the politics to others.

Joan appeared at his office door and ushered him to the biocontainment area where they dressed in their Blue suits. The monkey room was not attached to the main Level 4 laboratory, and the two scientists unplugged their air hoses, shuffled down a small corridor, and entered the monkey room. The animals squealed and rattled their cages. Rows of numbered steel cages along the walls faced a large table in the center of the room. The walls were concrete blocks painted white. Monkey biscuits were scattered on the concrete floor. The researchers reached for an air hose, plugged in, and moved to the cages. Zolowsky jumped backwards when a monkey shot a hand through the bars. Joan reassured him that the animals couldn't break through the heavy bolts on the cages.

Four groups of two monkeys would be used in the experiment. Group 1, the control group, would receive nothing. Group 2 would get only the GSE antidote. Joan had decided to add this group since Matt had injected the HIS-mice with the antidote and they survived with no problems, and she wanted to determine if it produced the same result in the monkey. Group 3 would be infected with only the St. Louis virus, and group 4 would be infected with the virus and after thirty minutes would be treated with the GSE protein.

"ARE YOU READY?" shouted Joan.

Zolowsky nodded.

Working with monkeys wasn't easy, but the researchers had the experience—Joan more than he. Handling a dead monkey was even worse.

When they had finished the inoculations, Joan looked up at the clock.

"IT'S NOON. THE THIRTY MINUTES ARE UP. LET'S INJECT GROUP FOUR WITH THE ANTIDOTE."

After another thirty minutes, the researchers observed the animals as they passed in front of the cages. Suddenly, each of the two group 3 monkeys infected with only the virus fell over and bled from the mouth. Animals in the other cages seemed okay for the time being.

"WE NEED TO REMOVE THESE MONKEYS TO THE NECROPSY ROOM BEFORE THEY TURN TO MUSH," shouted Zolowsky.

Joan cautioned him. They had to make sure the monkeys were dead. Sometimes an infected animal that appears dead can wake up. They had sharp teeth and powerful jaws that could do much damage. A bite from an infected animal would be fatal to the researcher. The animals' faces were deformed and eyes bloody. There was no question; these monkeys were dead. They placed them in special containers and took them to the necropsy table. Zolowsky quickly took several tissue samples and stored them. Then he followed Joan to the monkey room to mercy kill one of the group 4 monkeys treated with the virus and the antidote, and took it to the post-mortem room. Joan performed an autopsy, and Zolowsky took tissue samples.

"YOU CAN TAKE THE SAMPLES TO THE EM WHILE I FINISH HERE," said Joan.

"YOU SURE?"

She nodded.

Later that afternoon, she returned to the monkey room.

"Oh, my God!" shouted Joan.

The group 1 monkeys—the control group—were sitting down with watery eyes and bloody noses.

Minutes later, they fell over dead.

———◆———

Zolowsky sat at the electron microscope dressed in green scrubs. He looked up from the micrographs when Joan entered the microscopy lab, dressed in scrubs.

"Something scary happened," she said.

He frowned.

"The control group bled out."

Zolowsky's eyes widened. "Transmission from one sick animal to a healthy one."

"We knew it was an airborne virus, but I guess we should have known it could be transmitted from animal to animal."

"That would mean many more deaths," said Zolowsky.

He reached for the micrographs. "Look at these."

She took the top one and studied it. "This looks like the St. Louis virus before it mutates. Just like what I saw weeks ago."

"Now look at this one."

She studied it. "That's the mutant."

He nodded again. "Now look at this."

"This…" She stopped and stared at it. "There are only pieces. Whatever it is, most of it is gone." She paused, studying it more closely. "Are you trying to trick me?"

"Not at all. It's from the group 4 monkey. The antidote dissolved the virus, keeping it from mutating."

———◆———

Back in her office, Joan flipped open her cell phone and called Matt

"Where are you?" she asked.

"Rosen's, having a sandwich."

"We need to talk."

"What happened?"

"I'll be right there," she said.

Twenty minutes later, Joan walked into the deli and found Matt in the back booth. Mr. Rosen stood by the table with a white apron around his waist and a pot of coffee in his hand. No wonder Matt likes this place, she thought. He gets a lot of attention.

Mr. Rosen smiled as he passed her. She slid in the seat opposite

Matt. Half a sandwich lay on his plate and a full cup of coffee next to it.

"You really like this place, don't you?"

"Tell me—did it work?"

She reached across the table, placing her hand on his. "Matt, it's the greatest, and it didn't make the monkeys sick. The same results you found in the HIS-mice."

He nearly jumped out of his seat. "Thank God. Thank God," he said, grabbing both of her hands. "Now we have something to fight the general with." Then he frowned. Apparently he sensed something or saw something in her eyes. "What's wrong? It didn't last. Did it? The virus broke through." He held his breath.

She shook her head. "No, no. That's not it."

"Then what?"

"Has nothing to do with your antidote."

"Then what the hell is it?"

"The control group bled out."

"Is that all?" He sighed.

"But that magnifies the problem. Omega Bytes stays around for ten days."

He shook his head. "Ten days?"

"How much antidote do you have?" she asked.

Instead of responding, he looked away.

"What's wrong?"

"We had over fifty doses."

"Had?"

"Twenty-five were stolen after DnaTech received permission from Jagger to mass-produce it."

"That's when the general learned the antidote was ready," she said.

He nodded. "And had someone steal it from my lab."

"The general's moving very fast," she said.

"We've got to find out what's going on," said Matt.

CHAPTER FORTY-TWO

Matt had asked Peter to remain behind in the conference room after they finished reviewing the data from the monkey experiments with Joan. He had something he wanted to discuss with him.

"It's time we broach the subject of terrorism."

Peter frowned. "Terrorism? I don't understand."

"Taylor and Mors. They're involved in an organization called APAT. They're terrorists as far as I'm concerned. Ever hear of APAT?"

Peter surprised Matt by telling him he learned about the organization from *60 Minutes*. Two *Washington Post* reporters tried to infiltrate the organization when an informant called the paper and told them APAT was meeting in an abandoned shipyard building in Virginia. The reporters went, set up their cameras, and waited. The meeting never took place. Peter suggested that Taylor had the APAT members' phones bugged and notified Mors. The informant may have been a major in the Air Force. He was found dead soon after.

"Taylor's in Intelligence," said Matt, "he could have assassinated the guy."

"The DIA has an incredible intelligence network," said Peter.

Matt knew the composition of APAT from the documents he stole from Taylor's office, but was appalled when he had read that some of the members were scientists. Peter reminded him that scientists were patriotic people, too, who also had political missions. Many didn't hide in their labs.

"But APAT's mission is outside the law."

"Doesn't matter, if the cause is great enough," said Peter.

"Then they're terrorists."

Matt was taken aback by Peter's passion in support of the scientist.

He had to ask. "Are you or were you one of them?"

Peter's eyes widened. "I knew you'd figure it out eventually."

"I'd like to know about your involvement to get a feel for the organization."

"A foolish thing I did."

Matt considered Peter Crane to be not only a colleague, but also a good friend. Chris had told him that APAT used powerful recruiting tools to recruit members, dealing with the failures of the CIA, the FBI and even the Congress in Homeland Security.

Peter explained that a friend at USAMRIID invited him for a round of golf to tell him about APAT. Peter got so worked up when he heard about the government's ineffectiveness in Homeland Security that he decided to attend an APAT meeting with his friend. At first Peter liked their mission: to keep the government agencies on their toes. But when he learned they had talked about combat training, capturing and executing terrorists, he dropped out.

"Did you ever see General Taylor and Mors at any of the meetings?"

"I only went to three meetings. Taylor was there, but this Mors person talked to us over *The Box*, a telephone hookup. We never saw him."

"Did Taylor ever see you?"

He shook his head. "Too many of us."

"Did anyone ever ask about Mors?"

"No. Maybe they were afraid too. We just knew he was the big man. Even Taylor seemed intimidated by his voice. Usually, the big shots met separately from us."

"Big shots?"

"I heard they had bigwigs on the board," said Peter.

"Then why did you come to DnaTech when Taylor asked you?"

"Once you work for Taylor, you can't get out. I'm sure you've figured out that most of the people at the Center had come from Detrick."

Both fell silent. Then Matt said, "I need to ask you something, and I want the truth."

Peter's eyes narrowed. "Okay."

"The FBI has determined that the handwriting on the last page of the *Red Book* matches yours. Which tells me you sent the *Red Book* to Jack, probably thinking he would use it to discredit the general. Correct?"

"You must believe me. I'm really sorry."

"Sorry? Dammit! You put Jack in grave danger."

"Jack had so much passion for doing the right thing; I thought he'd give it to Devlin. Didn't think he'd blab his fool head off."

Peter lowered his head. Matt thought he had seen tears in his eyes.

"I was afraid," he said, looking up, staring into Matt's eyes. "Someone sent it to me while I was at Detrick. I didn't know what to do with it. I wanted someone to have it—in case they killed me."

CHAPTER FORTY-THREE

Many researchers complained that their lab imprisoned them, but not Joan Wu, she felt comfortable in there. She rose, reached for her light raincoat, looked around the office as if to say good night, and flipped off the lights. She rode the elevator to the first floor and stopped at the sliding glass doors at the south end, when she saw the driving rain. She stepped outside, stood under the canopy, listened as the raindrops smacked the metal, and held her head down to avoid the sheets of wind-blown rain. After several minutes, the rain lessened, but ominous black clouds roiled in the sky. Joan took off running to her white Nissan Maxima and moved out of the parking space to join a line of slow moving vehicles, waiting for the guard to wave them through the gate. Joan approached the junction of Clayton and Hanley roads and maneuvered onto Hanley Road, heading north.

She arrived at Matt's townhouse, turned in, and parked next to his BMW. After leaving her car, she stopped a few minutes to admire the stars in the evening sky. The rain had stopped, and the clouds had moved out. She inhaled the crisp air, and exhaled. *It's such a beautiful night.*

———— ◆ ————

The doorbell sounded just as Matt shoved the salad into the fridge. He looked at the wall clock. It was almost seven-thirty. She's on time, he thought.

"I'm coming, Joan," he said as he opened the door. She smiled and moved past him, stopping in the foyer.

"Let me have your raincoat," he said, placing it in the hall closet.

"Something smells good," she said.

"Lamb," he said, touching her shoulder to guide her to the breakfast bar. "Have a seat. I'll get you some wine." "The Way You Look Tonight" resonated in the room from his disk player. Matt liked the oldies.

"That'll be enough for now," she said, placing a finger at the half-full mark, as Matt poured the Chablis.

He then looked into the top oven, reached in, removed a tray of warm hors d'oeuvres and placed the tray in front of her. "Help yourself while I finish dinner."

"My, you never cooked for me at Detrick," she said, taking a small roll of ham-wrapped prawn from the tray.

"When in grad school, I often visited a high school friend that was the chef at a French restaurant."

"It seems I don't know everything about you," she said.

He stood in the kitchen with a white towel fixed around his waist and glanced at Joan, wondering how she really felt about him. She caught him looking at her, and he smiled. He knew that if her brother Kenny had left them alone, they'd probably be married by now.

"What are you thinking?" she asked. Her black hair glistened in the light, and her brown eyes sparkled.

"About how lovely you look."

She raised her wineglass.

Matt raised his glass, then took a sip, and set it on the counter next to the stove.

"You're just as organized in the kitchen as in your lab. I can't believe it," she said. "Not anal retentive, just organized."

He knew where it came from. His mother. She even scrubbed the concrete stoop in the front of their home. His dad tracked in mud from the fields, which nearly drove her crazy. But Matt never did. She'd kill him.

"My mother. She taught me how to get things done."

He moved into the den to light the candles on a table dressed with a white tablecloth and a setting of china. A metal ice bucket with a bottle of wine was at the edge of the table. He smiled at her, as he returned to the kitchen. *I hope she likes the meal.*

"Let me help you," she said, sliding off the stool and moving into the kitchen.

Matt removed the salad from the fridge, placed it on the counter, and then pulled down the top oven door and yanked out the hot bread. "How about putting some salad into the bowls and this bread in that basket," he said, pointing, "and place them on the table and then take a seat."

"Glad to," she said.

Matt opened the lower oven, pulled a covered pan from it, removed the lid and transferred the *Novarin d'agneau*—leg of lamb, laced with garlic and rubbed with olive oil and fresh rosemary—to a platter. On the back burner was a casserole of eggplant, tomatoes, onions, peppers and zucchini.

Matt transferred the food to the table.

Joan straightened in her chair and said, "Hmmm… this is going to be good."

He refilled her wineglass. Matt motioned for her to begin.

"Delicious," she said. "Thanks for inviting me."

"I was surprised you accepted my invitation."

She set her fork on her plate. "Why?"

"I don't know… I sensed you're still pissed at me."

She reached for her wineglass, took a sip, and eyed him over the rim of the glass.

"Are you?" he asked.

"I'm not sure."

"What kind of answer is that?"

"That depends on you."

Women, he thought, you can't ever please them. "You mean if I'm a good boy."

She rolled her eyes. "That isn't what I meant, and you know it." She paused, thinking about something.

"How do you feel about Kenny?"

"Does that mean he's still running your life?"

Matt could see the darts blasting from her eyes.

"And if he were?"

"I had hoped you had grown the past two years, and we wouldn't worry about him anymore. Get back to the way we were in Maryland before he came into the picture."

"Maybe." She twirled the stem of her wineglass next to her plate and stared at it before saying, "You heard about Sergeant Marlowe?"

"Peter told me. It's worse than a slatewiper."

"It was awful," she said, shaking her head. "His body dissolved before my eyes. I'll never forget it."

Matt waited until she wiped the tears with her napkin before saying, "Of course, you know it was no accident."

She nodded. "Max saw Ash leave the room during the test and believes he stopped the air to Marlowe's hose."

"Ash again," said Matt with disgust in his voice. "He's everywhere."

"I think someone's following me."

Matt set his fork on his plate.

"You don't seem surprised," said Joan. "Am I missing something?"

"Ash has been following me for months."

Her eyes widened. "You never mentioned it."

"Wasn't important until now."

"Do you think he's dangerous?" she asked.

"I doubt that he'd hurt you, if that's what you mean. But Taylor must have something planned for us down the road."

She leaned in. "What?"

"How do I know?" He reached for a roll. "They've probably been watching you ever since I came."

"Because they know we were lovers at Detrick?"

"Yes."

"I'm getting scared."

"What happened to that strong-willed major I used to know?"

"Just because I'm an officer, doesn't mean I'm not human," she said. "What... are we to do?"

"Stop them."

She frowned. "How?"

"Destroy the microchips."

She gasped. "Destroy them?"

"You said they're stored in Max's lab. Right?"

"Yes, but... you're suggesting that we break in?"

He nodded, and then wiped his mouth with his napkin.

"Have you gone psycho?"

"There's no one else. Remember that wall of secrecy?"

"You know what they'll do to us, if we're caught? And they'd get away with it."

"Not this time."

"Why are you so cocky?"

"Can't tell you just yet," he said, thinking about Chris Cousins.

He thought about how much of a rush he got when he broke into General Taylor's office. Was he becoming overconfident, arrogant? He didn't think so. Arrogance would blind him, and he still hadn't lost sight of reality.

"We'll do it tomorrow night."

"Tomorrow night? That soon?"

Matt nodded.

Moments later, he rose and stepped away from the table, carrying his dish and glass to the kitchen.

"I'll put on some coffee," he said.

Once the table had been cleared, the area cleaned and the dishes put away, Matt filled two cups with coffee and carried them into the living room. Joan chose the couch, and Matt placed the cups on the coffee table and slid in next to her. He watched as she reached for her cup and sipped the coffee. He regarded her in a truly loving way while a warm feeling flowed over him. When she set her cup down, he moved closer to her and put his arm around her shoulder, pressing his face against hers and said, "I still love you." His lips brushed her ear. "I want everything to be like before," he said, and he pulled her to him.

Joan winced, and shouted, "Don't!"

He had expected her to melt in his arms, but instead, she drew back and scowled. Surprised, he backed away.

"I'm not ready for this," she said.

CHAPTER FORTY-FOUR

They slipped into the corridor around one in the morning, dressed in green surgical gowns, caps and rubber gloves, each holding a Mini Maglite flashlight like those used by crime-scene investigators.

Joan followed close behind Matt, moving toward the north end steps. The ceiling lights had been dimmed for the night. Holding on to his hand like a leash, she descended the stairs behind him and prayed that they wouldn't collide with anyone from the Surveillance Center.

They left the last step, moving through a curtain of darkness. Joan's heart began to race, and her breathing became difficult. She wondered if Matt was scared, too. Inching forward, they stayed close to the wall, sliding a hand against it. About a third of the way down the corridor, Matt pulled her into one of the niches that led into a lab. His back landed against the door, and her body pounded the front of him.

"What's wrong?" she whispered into his ear.

"Something up ahead."

In his embrace, she felt his breath on her face and his heart racing in his chest.

Beads of sweat formed on her forehead. She couldn't help but think about what would happen to them, if caught. She laid her head on Matt's shoulder. Seconds later, he moved her to one side and peered around the edge of the wall.

"Whatever it was, it's gone."

"Maybe it was one of the workers in the Surveillance Center."

He didn't comment on her hypothesis; instead, he grabbed her hand and inched along the wall again. She trusted Matt to get her to Max's lab in the darkness, because he had counted the number of steps from the stairs to the lab earlier that day. He had told her about his adventure into Ash's office, looking for the tapes, but it didn't make her feel any more confident in him.

"We're coming close to the Surveillance Center," said Matt.

Suddenly, the door to the center bolted open with a bang and a gush of light shot into the corridor, illuminating the area in front of the door. Matt and Joan slammed their backs against the wall and held their breaths. And waited. No one came out. What's going on, she thought. The door slammed shut with a bang, like on a timing mechanism, and the light vanished.

"Thank God," she whispered to Matt.

He didn't respond, but continued inching forward, this time sliding his right shoulder against the wall. Fifteen steps later, Matt turned the handle and pulled hard on the door to the Level 2. They moved into the lab, and Joan pulled the door shut. Both reached for their Mini Maglite flashlights and directed the beams to the floor next to the wall. Matt stopped in the back of the room.

"Look in the freezer against the wall," she said, pointing her flashlight in that direction. Her palms grew clammy watching Matt going to it. He lifted the door, and a cloud of condensation billowed into his face. The instant she saw him open the freezer, a wave of acid welled up from her stomach. She had expected the overhead lights to flash on, and Taylor and Ash to jump out at them. She inhaled a deep breath and watched Matt direct his flashlight beam inside the freezer.

"It's empty," he said just over a whisper.

She moved to his side, circled her flashlight inside the freezer, over two shelves layered with ice. "Of course. They wouldn't leave them so vulnerable. What was I thinking?"

"Obviously, they've moved them," said Matt. "Do you know of any other place?"

"No, dammit!"

"Well, look around for Chrissake. You take that wall over there," he said, pointing. "I'll take this one. Look for a door in the wall."

A few minutes later, Joan whispered, "I found something."

Matt rushed to her.

"I nearly missed it," she said. "It's got a lock on it."

"I'll cut it off," said Matt, reaching for a tool on his belt and worked it on the lock.

"But they'll know we broke into it," she said.

"Who cares?"

"I do."

"What's taking you so long?" she asked.

"Do you want to do it?"

"I just asked."

Matt worked the cutting tool harder and finally the lock snapped open. Joan pulled the door open.

"It's empty," she shouted.

"Whatever they've got planned, they're ready," said Matt.

CHAPTER FORTY-FIVE

Matt had stopped in front of Rosen's Deli. He had a good run, averaging an eight-minute mile. His gray T-shirt had streaks of sweat. The dry wind sent electrical sensations over his skin that invigorated him. He kept running in place to keep the endorphins circulating. Few cars parked on Hanley Road at seven in the morning, yet the silver Buick sedan parked half a block away.

He mumbled to himself, and turned and hurried in the opposite direction. He stopped to glance over his shoulder.

The car lunged forward, then stopped. Matt ran for a block, then stopped to look back. The sedan sped toward him, then stopped. *They mean business.*

He took off running, darted into an alley, jumped a fence like a hurdler, and stopped among a grove of trees in a small park. His heart hammered against his rib cage, and he labored to catch his breath.

He glanced around a large tree a half block from his townhouse. The sedan, parked one hundred feet away, looked like a 16-wheeler. Its engine revved at him. He couldn't see any faces, but he made out Ash's silhouette on the passenger's side.

He waited. The he peered around the tree again. The engine revved again. The noise from the engine challenged him, but his knees shook.

They know we broke into Max's lab.

The urge to dash across the street became strong, but that's what they wanted.

He waited. They waited. Could he make it? He wiped his forehead with his sleeve, while running in place to keep up his courage. *I think I can make it. If only this tree were closer to the street. By the time I run to the street they could be on me.* Suddenly, with a surge of energy he sprinted off like a running back heading for the end zone. His fear left him. He glanced over his left shoulder.

The sedan's wheels spun, spitting a plume of white smoke into the air, and squealed like a raging dinosaur.

"The goal line is near," he cried.

Adrenaline ripped through his veins. He gave it all he had.

"I'm going to make it!" he screamed.

Inches from the curb, the silver sedan caught him on his thigh, spun him around like a tornado until he slammed against a tree in the yard.

--------◆--------

"Dr. Brenner, can you hear me?"

Matt opened his eyes. *There's a ghost in my dream standing by my side.*

"I'm dreaming," he said.

"You're not dreaming," said the young doctor dressed in white.

"Who are you?"

"I'm your doctor. Dr. Forrester. You're one lucky dude."

"Do you know what happened to you?" asked someone.

The voice was familiar to Matt.

"No. Who are you?"

"Joan."

"Joan? Where am I?"

"St. Mary's Hospital."

Matt closed his eyes. Joan and Dr. Forrester waited.

"They hit me, didn't they?" Matt took a deep breath. "Did they catch them?"

"I'm afraid not," said the doctor. He turned to Joan. "A detective interviewed the only witness, who said a silver sedan hit him, but no one got a license number or description of the occupants. There were tire marks for twenty feet." Then he gestured for Joan to follow him outside the curtain.

"Dr. Brenner will be released in a few hours. He has several lacerations on his arms and legs, and a nasty bruise on his left thigh. We've taken care of the lacerations, but he'll need to rest a couple of weeks. Make sure he stays off that leg." Dr. Forrester shook his head. "He's a very lucky man."

Joan returned to Matt's side and whispered into his ear, "The doctor said it was a silver Buick. Isn't that Ash?"

"Could be. Could be DIA."

"They know what we did," said Joan. "I'm scared."
"It's time for you to meet someone," said Matt.

CHAPTER FORTY-SIX

"Who are we waiting for?" said Joan, carrying two cups of tea from the kitchen into the living room of Matt's townhouse. Ever since Matt told her about meeting someone at seven o'clock that evening, she had been racking her brain.

Matt didn't respond right away. He sat in the overstuffed chair, rubbing his thigh. "Someone important." He sighed. "Cut down on the chatter. I'm trying to get through this pain until the painkillers kick in."

She placed a cup in front of him, then moved to the couch, setting her cup on the coffee table. She took a sip of tea and stared at Matt. He laid his head back and closed his eyes. Irritation swept over her. He was treating her like a child. *Why doesn't he just come out and tell me who it is if this person is so damn important?* Which one of Matt's friends could it be? She moved forward. "I know who it is. It's your Stanford friend, Dr. Keyes." She had solved the mystery, and it felt good. "It's Dr. Keyes."

Matt didn't respond.

The doorbell jolted her. She rose, went to the door, opened it, and stared at the handsome round face with dark brown eyes and short black beard. *This can't be Dr. Keyes. He's too young.* She hadn't expected a man so handsome, and one who knew how to dress. *Matt could learn a few things from him.*

He passed in front of her. "I'm Chris Cousins," he said, holding out his hand.

She grasped it and took a moment to stare into his smiling eyes. She blushed and withdrew her hand. "I'm Joan Wu. Matt's in the living room."

"I know the way. I've been here before."

"Can't get up," said Matt, pointing to his thigh. "It hurts too much."

Chris chose to sit at the end of the couch next to Matt. "I'm glad you called me."

Joan took a seat at the other end of the couch.

"How are you feeling?" asked Chris. "I mean, what did the doctor say?"

Matt waved it off as nothing. "I'll be okay. They hit me in the thigh. Doc said I have to stay off it for a few days—"

"A few weeks," interrupted Joan. "The doctor said a few weeks, not a few days."

"We knew that something like this might happen," said Chris. "Frankly, I thought it would have happened sooner."

Matt frowned. "So you expected all along that they'd get me like they did that APAT informant?"

"No way. I meant I thought they'd try something creative, like releasing some deadly bug in your lab." He quickly added, "Of course, I knew you'd be able to handle it."

Who is this guy? What are they talking about? "Excuse me," said Joan. "Matt you haven't introduced us."

Chris shot a conspiratorial look at Matt. "You haven't told her?"

Matt forced a smile. "Joan, this is Special Agent Chris Cousins. He's with the FBI."

She blinked with incredulity. "The FBI?"

"Matt's been working for us."

Feeling much better since the painkillers had kicked in, Matt turned to Joan. "I guess you're wondering why I never told you."

"You bet I am."

"We thought it best he didn't tell anyone," said Chris. "General Taylor could have gotten wind of it."

"Well, it didn't work. Matt could have been killed."

"That's because I stirred the waters, going to Ellisville. I brought this on myself. It's not Chris' fault."

"We needed Matt to gather evidence against General Taylor, who's one of the leaders of an organization called APAT."

"Don't forget Mors," added Matt.

He nodded. "Mors is their leader. We're looking for him."

Joan turned to Chris. "So, did Matt get what you wanted?"

Matt looked at Chris.

"He did."

"And?" said Joan.

"Can't discuss it. Top Secret."

"I see. Does Matt's accident mean that...?" She couldn't get herself to finish the sentence.

"That they tried to kill me?"

"We'll be on Matt twenty-four-seven."

"You haven't answered my question. Will Taylor try to hurt Matt again?"

"We can only surmise he will. We'll do everything in our power to prevent that."

"Your protection isn't worth shit. Look at him. Where were you guys?"

"Touché. It won't happen again."

Joan felt a mixture of anger and fear. She was angry over a fellow officer who stood for all the wrong things, and she feared him, knowing that he had something planned for her.

"I'm being followed, too."

Chris nodded like he had known.

"Do you think they'll come after me?"

"You're an officer, so he'll treat you differently. I'm confident he's planning something."

"You must protect her," said Matt.

"We'll do our best. But we have to be realistic."

"Is there anything I should do?" said Joan.

"We think Colonel Jagger can be trusted, but I wouldn't approach him just yet. Go about your business. We're watching Ash and the general."

———— ✦ ————

After Chris had left, Matt moved to the couch.

"Easy," said Joan as Matt slid in next to her. "Watch that leg."

"Pain's gone for now. The medicine is working well."

Matt lay his head back and turned to look into Joan's soft brown eyes.

"What?" she said.

"His remark. It shook me up. I couldn't stand it if anything happened to you."

"I'll be okay. I've got you." His gaze locked on hers. This act of bravery wasn't fooling him. He could see the fear in her eyes.

He pushed her back on the couch and almost covered her with his body. She didn't resist. He knew she felt his male hardness against her thighs. Her arms went around his neck as she closed her eyes. He had been waiting for this moment for two years. Starved for the taste of her lips, he went for her mouth. As he ran his hands over her smooth body, she began to moan.

Minutes later, her warm naked body lay under him. He kissed her all over, and she moaned and jerked with each kiss. She opened her soft brown eyes, displaying a warmth and sincere look of honest desire for him. He now realized how much she loved him.

CHAPTER FORTY-SEVEN

Captain Ash flipped open his cell phone, then shut it. He didn't want to make this call. Lately, General Taylor exploded over the slightest infraction, and Ash made it a point to stay out of his way. But he had to report on Brenner's accident before DIA beat him to it. He inhaled a deep breath and opened his cell phone, hoping the general wasn't in his Pentagon office. He heard a click and Taylor answered. "Yes?"

"Dr. Brenner and Major Wu entered Dr. Tandenbaum's lab early yesterday morning, sir." That isn't what he wanted to say. His hand shook.

"What the hell are you worried about? We have the chips."

Ash remembered how pleased the general was when he occluded Sergeant Marlowe's air hose, so he brought it up again to ingratiate himself with the general. "I bet the major still hasn't figured out how I took care of Marlowe."

"She knows."

"You're right, sir. She's smart."

When Ash learned that Brenner and Wu had snuck into Max's lab, looking for the microchips, he lost it and decided he'd teach Brenner a lesson. He couldn't let a civilian put one over on the Army and get away with it.

The general snorted in the phone. "What do you want? I'm busy."

"Sir..." Ash paused to assemble his courage. "Brenner... he's had an accident."

"ACCIDENT?" shouted Taylor.

"Hit by a car. But he's okay. Just wanted to scare him, sir."
Oh, shit. Here it comes. The hammer.

"You're an idiot. I told you I had something special planned for him and the bitch."

"General? Brenner's just a little banged up. He's okay."

"He better be." He paused. "Did you get the antidote?"

"A piece of cake. Twenty-five doses."

CHAPTER FORTY-EIGHT

The helicopter set down at HT-Systems around seven in the morning. A multi-billion dollar company in Maryland with top-secret security clearance, HT-Systems existed on government contracts and guarded its clandestine dealings from the media. The media had reported that HT-Systems employees, thought to be secret agents, carried guns. The Pentagon knew it was a front for the CIA to ship arms, high technology equipment and computers overseas, and couldn't care less. They needed HT-Systems.

Three federal agents, two men and one woman, met General Taylor at the helipad and escorted him away from the chopper. Encircled by the agents, holding a leather case close to his chest, he said, "Let's get to the computer lab."

Taylor followed them to a white stucco building without windows. The two men opened a large metal door at the end of the building and held it open for the general as he and the female agent passed by them. They proceeded through a narrow corridor with exposed overhead fluorescent lighting and unpainted white sheetrock walls. This place is a dump, Taylor thought.

The agents led him into a large room with long tables, a glass-enclosed office in the corner where they left him with a corporal seated behind a desk.

"I'm Corporal Cecil Williams, sir," he said, jumping to his feet, standing at attention. Cecil was a computer genius, in his late twenties, thin, with brown hair that needed combing, and he wore a white T-shirt that had "Genius" printed on the front.

He's just a kid, the general thought. What does he know?

"Sit," said the general. "Where are you from, Corporal?"

"Alabama, sir," said Williams with a drawl. "Born and reared in the south. Going back when I get out of this man's Army."

"Not just for men anymore," said Taylor.

Williams nodded. "I know, sir."

Taylor glanced through a window into the next room. Computers were sitting on a wooden bench. "So you know computers?"

"Been playing with 'em ever since I was no higher than this." Cecil extended his hand out to his side about two feet from the floor. "My dad owns a database company in Auburn, the largest in the south, sir."

I didn't know anything good came out of Alabama.

"Do you have the computers ready?"

"Yes sir. Been waiting for you." He rose from his chair, reached for the leather case Taylor held out to him, and moved into the adjacent room.

"These two computers are going to the Middle East as you instructed," said Cecil, waving his hand over them.

After thirty minutes, he completed inserting the microchips and the slender boards into the computers.

"What are you doing?" asked Taylor, standing next to the corporal, peering into the computer.

"Adjusting the settings on the chipboards so they'll recognize the commands. Whoever developed them is a genius."

After finishing the adjustments on the electronics board, Cecil turned to the general, and said, "One thing, sir?"

"Yes corporal?"

"I've studied the electronics on the Omega Bytes board and was wondering..." his voice dropped.

"What is it?"

"Using a remote control to release the virus would be much better, sir. With the satellites today, you can release the virus anywhere with a remote, but the boards were designed only for the Internet. If the terrorists don't plug the computers in, Omega Bytes is useless."

Taylor rubbed his chin. *He's right. They might not turn the computer on for some time.* He took a deep breath. "The word on your T-shirt fits you, Corporal."

"Thank you, sir."

"Corporal, you've given me a computer that can kill even if it sits in a box or on someone's desk."

"Doesn't matter where it is, sir. It's like a bomb ready to be detonated."

"How long will it take to make the adjustments to a remote control?"

"About two weeks, sir."

"Go to it."

CHAPTER FORTY-NINE

APAT had just finished a military exercise and had gathered in their building located in the woods somewhere in Virginia. They had been practicing their military maneuvers in full combat dress and with weapons. Mors, their leader, addressed the group through the "Box."

"Gentlemen? The general has informed me that al-Qaeda has established foothold in a warehouse in Newark."

"It's time to move in," said the retired FBI agent.

"They're gathering at nine-thirty next Friday evening," said Mors.

"We've been training," said the Air Force Colonel. "We're ready, sir."

"General Taylor will give you your orders," said Mors.

The timing was incredible. No sooner had Mors' voice left the Box when a voice blasted them from a bullhorn outside.

"This is the FBI. You're surrounded. Come out with your hands behind your heads."

CHAPTER FIFTY

General Taylor's cell phone vibrated in his pocket as he drove into his parking space at the Pentagon. He flipped it open. An Air Force Colonel on the run informed him that the FBI had surrounded the APAT camp and rounded up everyone.

"Son of a bitch!" screamed Taylor.

Arriving in his office Taylor reached for the red phone.

"Mors here."

"Just got word that the FBI has encircled our camp and are taking everyone into custody," said Taylor.

"Shit!"

Silence for a few moments. Then Mors asked, "What's our backup plan, Princeton?"

"Only thing left to do." He paused. "Release the biological on the bastards."

"Princeton. We don't have enough antidote."

"We can't wait. Al-Qaeda's meeting in a few days, and then all hell will break loose in this country."

"Princeton, get hold of yourself! Let the FBI go after them."

"THEY WON'T," shouted Taylor, breaking the circuit.

CHAPTER FIFTY-ONE

Corporal Cecil Williams nearly jumped out of his skin when he heard the phone ring. He set his coffee cup on the bench and grabbed the phone on the third ring. *It's probably the general.*

"Corporal Williams, sir," he said.

"Hey Cecil, this is Buddy."

Cecil and Buddy Long, two friends from Alabama, had joined the Army together.

"Hey Buddy. I thought you were the general."

"I've got something strange to tell you about him."

"What?" said Cecil after realizing he was holding his breath.

"The general's been feeding us some bull about a computer that can kill people."

"The general?" said Cecil, surprised. "When did you see him?"

"This morning during a briefing."

Buddy was DIA.

"The general's talking about inserting a killer computer into some warehouse. You're the computer genius. Tell me, how can a computer kill people?"

The corporal's head pounded. He realized the general never intended to ship the computers to the Middle East.

"Hold on a minute," said Cecil, putting the phone down. He went into the next room. One of the Omega Bytes computers was gone. His heart raced. *The general didn't trust me. He won't get this one.*

Cecil returned to his office and grabbed the phone. "Sorry about that. Where were we? Oh, yeah. Computers don't kill. Hell, that's crazy talk. Taylor likes to impress people with bullshit."

"I don't know. He seemed serious."

"It's nothing but an experimental computer with a high tech mini-camera. It processes pictures in great detail, then shoots them to the Pentagon. He wants pictures to keep track of al-Qaeda's movements. That's all."

"A computer with a high tech mini-camera? How's it we've never heard of it in Intelligence?"

"Top Secret shit in the Pentagon."

"But we're DIA," said Buddy.

"Trust me on this." Cecil knew Buddy wasn't buying it.

"Okay, if you say so, but you better watch your back."

"Why would I do that?"

"I heard the general tell some fat captain to take care of some unfinished business back at HT-Systems. The captain smiled like he knew what the general meant. Did he mean you?"

———— • ————

Cecil Williams called Max Tandenbaum to tell him that General Taylor had taken an Omega Bytes Computer and was going to place it in some warehouse. He didn't know where.

"How about when?" said Max, spitting out the words in contempt.

"Probably in a week. I can't be party to his madness, that's why I called."

"Where's he now?"

"He said he'd be here today, but I doubt if I'll ever see him again."

"What do you mean?"

"I'm making myself scarce."

Since removing the chips from his lab and delivering them to Taylor, Max had become anxious and despondent. He had been hitting the bottle, hard. He felt like he had invented something worse than the hydrogen bomb. Yet, Cecil may have given him his redemption. Max said, "We need to find the computer and remove it before he sets it off."

"That won't work," said Cecil. "I modified your board so the virus could be activated by remote control."

Max snorted. His redemption had vanished.

Cecil took a deep breath. "If the terrorists didn't plug the computer in or turn it on, your chip wouldn't have been worth a shit."

"You're as crazy as the general."

"Hey, you're the one who created the evil thing."

Max slammed the phone on its base, thinking about what he had done. Cecil was right. At this moment he felt like one of God's rejects. Who could he turn to for help? No one. Everyone hated him, and for good reason. He thought about calling Major Wu, but asking a woman for help with his problem was beneath him. He chewed on his lower lip for a few seconds and then made the call.

———•———

Stunned, Joan looked across the room as she hung up the phone.

"Can you do anything to stop him?" Max had asked her. She knew that it took a lot of effort on his part to ask for her help, like moving a mountain. She felt a prickling sensation up her spine when she thought about what General Taylor had planned.

Matt Brenner entered her office.

"What's so important that it couldn't wait until morning?"

Joan motioned for him to take a seat.

"Are you okay? You look a little pale."

"I've learned something that has me pretty scared." She took a deep breath. "Got a call from Max. Some corporal at HT-Systems has been working with the general on the Omega Bytes board, and he has changed it to work off a remote control." She paused. "Worse yet, Taylor's going to release the virus somewhere, but no one knows where or when."

Matt bolted from his chair and began pacing the room. "The crazy bastard will do it. You can bet on it." He shook his head. "We've only got forty doses of the antidote."

"What about DnaTech?" she asked.

"Won't have enough for several months."

"Better alert Chris," she said.

CHAPTER FIFTY-TWO

Matt maneuvered his BMW through the streets of Clayton for an hour to unwind. He pulled into a side street facing the Hawaiian Club and parked with the motor running, watching the cars in his rearview and side-view mirrors as they passed, while at the same time keeping an eye on the club. After twenty minutes, he pulled into a parking place on the side of the building, away from the street, left his car and entered the club.

Two couples, seated at one of the front tables, didn't notice him as he passed them. One person sat at the bar drinking coffee and smoking a cigarette, watching a taped NBA game. The place smelled like a fish market. Ten-thirty in the morning was too early for the lunch crowd. Matt headed to the back of the dining area, dodging waiters, who had finished dressing the tables with white tablecloths. Once seated, he ordered a latte and waited, watching the front.

Chris came through the door.

"What do you have?" he asked.

A middle-aged man wearing a white shirt with rolled-up sleeves and a white apron fastened to his waist approached the table with a small pad in hand and a pen in the other. "What can I get you gentlemen?"

"Some coffee, black," said Chris.

"I'll take another latte," said Matt, pushing his cup toward the waiter.

Chris pulled out a chair and sat.

"Now, what's so important?"

"Max Tandenbaum got a call from Cecil Williams. You know who he is?"

Chris adjusted himself in his chair and watched the waiter place both coffee cups on the table and then leave. He took a couple of sips of coffee, then said, "He's a computer guru at HT-Systems. What did he want?"

"He's modified the electronics board in the Omega Bytes computer so it responds by remote control."

"Max told you this?"

"He told Joan, and she told me. Also, Taylor's taken the computer with him, and no one knows where."

"Our agents spotted him and Ash in Newark two weeks ago, but lost them."

"Do you think Newark's the target?"

"Al-Qaeda is operating an import-export business there as a front for recruiting and training militants. We've learned they plan to establish cells in four other cities to release WMDs."

Matt lunged forward almost coming out of his chair. "That's it. Taylor's going to release his slatewiper in that warehouse. You must arrest him now!"

"He's gone underground," said Chris.

"If you don't capture him, he's going to kill millions of people. Now that he has the remote, he could release his virus from anywhere."

"The general's Special Forces training has made him a formidable adversary. We've established a command center across from the warehouse, and he hasn't been seen."

"Then go after al-Qaeda."

He threw up his hands. "We've been instructed to keep hands off until they break the law."

"That'll be too damn late. Who in the hell told you that?"

"Who else... the White House."

"The White House? Man, you're the FBI. Screw the White House. Worry about them after you get al-Qaeda."

"Can't! It'd be my ass."

"I'd rather it be yours than millions of dead Americans. I'd think this one through, if I were you."

"We're going to do something. You and me."

"Hey, it's not my problem. I had nothing to do with the virus. I gave you what you wanted." He reached for his coffee, sipped it, then wiped his mouth with the napkin.

"You work for us now, so it's your problem, too," said Chris. "You're no Pontius Pilate. You can't wash your hands of this while millions of innocent people could die." He paused to catch his breath. "I need your help, Matt."

"You don't need me. Capture al-Qaeda."

"I just told you we can't. Even if we tried, Taylor'll release the virus. He wants to be the one to wipe them out."

They fell silent.

"We did capture APAT," said Chris.

Matt frowned. "When?"

"A few days ago. They were preparing to attack al-Qaeda, but we stopped them in time."

"Did you get Mors?"

"No. But we will."

"You know where you guys messed up?" said Matt. "You should have let APAT and al-Qaeda go at it."

Chris shook his head. "That's crazy talk. There would have been a massacre."

Matt wondered. If the INS allowed the terrorists to enter this country, and the FBI knew it, why did they allow al-Qaeda to get fortified in Newark?

"Tell me," said Matt, "how in the hell did you guys let them get such a stronghold in Newark in the first place? Is this another case of FBI screwing up big-time?"

Chris dodged the question. "Taylor has us over a barrel. We don't know where he is, and if we rush into the warehouse, he'd release his virus. He may be hiding in one of the buildings near the warehouse, watching us." He paused. "I know what you're thinking. We've searched all the buildings, but that doesn't mean anything. You're our only hope. You can dismantle the computer."

"Wait a minute. Have you forgotten about Max? Joan told me he's pissed at Taylor. He'd do it." Matt felt a weight fly off his shoulders. He knew Chris had to agree that Max was the person.

"Can't."

"Why not?"

"He's dead."

Matt scowled. "Dead?"

"He committed suicide. Ran off the road and hit a tree. Drunk. I got the call from headquarters on the way over here."

Matt was shrouded in uneasy feelings. He could be next. Maybe working with the FBI wasn't such a good idea after all, he thought. But then how could he avenge Jack's death? No, he did the right thing.

"So you weren't going to tell me about Max," said Matt.

"I just did."

Silence followed as the two men stared at each other, waiting for the other to say something.

"You didn't say anything until I brought up his name. You FBI guys are hard-nosed."

"Max's not our problem. Taylor and al-Qaeda are, and that's where you come in."

Matt saw faceless images floating across the top of his coffee. If they didn't do something, there'd be many Americans, not only without faces, but also without bodies.

Chris' gruff voice shook Matt from his thoughts. "Are you listening to me?"

"It's ironic, isn't it?" said Matt.

"What?"

"We have to save those bastards to save our own people."

"I'm afraid so. Now, back to what we have to do."

"I'm not an antiterrorist expert. I don't have any training."

"Don't need any. We'll be with you," said Chris. He finished off his coffee, and then leaned in. "There's no one else."

"Wait, just a minute. Cecil Williams. He's your man. I nearly forgot about him."

"We don't know where he is."

"Come on, that's baloney. You guys can find him."

"He's either in hiding or he's dead," said Chris.

Matt shook his head. "You know what this means? I'm next."

"For some reason, Taylor doesn't want you dead just yet," said Chris. "If he did, we'd know about it."

Matt felt his skin crawl. "I can't do it. Send in one of your counterterrorism experts."

"They wouldn't know how to disengage the damn thing."

"Bring it out, and I'll disarm it."

"Think straight," said Chris. "Our agents could do that. Taylor would set it off as they carted it out."

Matt's stomach knotted as he thought about Taylor. "He'll be watching for me, won't he?"

"We'll protect you."

"Bullshit! I know about your protection." Matt blinked hard. "I'll need some time to think about it."

"You've got twenty-four hours."

CHAPTER FIFTY-THREE

Matt returned to the Center around one-thirty, worked for an hour in his lab office, but found it difficult to concentrate. While he didn't see any of Taylor's men following him, he felt them watching him.

His hands shook as he lifted the phone to call Joan's cell number. No answer. He then called Rachel, Joan's secretary. Joan hadn't returned from lunch.

"I'm in my lab," he said. "Please have her call me once she comes in."

Matt asked Peter if he had seen her today. He saw her leaving the building with Colonel Jagger around eleven-thirty. Matt called the colonel's office. While he waited for Jagger to answer, Matt could feel his heart pounding.

"Don, did Joan go to lunch with you?"

"Yes, but she left before I did. Said she had to run by the Post Office. Anything wrong?"

"I can't reach her."

"I'm sure she's okay. Keep me informed." The phone went dead.

Matt took in a deep breath to calm himself. *Dammit, Joan, where are you?* He flinched when the phone rang.

"Dr. Brenner, there's a courier to see you," said Rachel.

"I'm not expecting any courier."

"He says it's important."

He sighed. "Okay. I'll meet him in the lunchroom."

A six-foot male dressed in Army green with sergeant stripes, sporting a crew cut, entered. "Are you Dr. Brenner?"

Matt nodded.

"Special letter for you, sir." The man's bulging upper arm muscles were like those of a wrestler's. *He's probably on steroids.*

Standing by one of the long tables close to the door, Matt reached for the envelope and thanked him. He returned to his office and stared at the envelope for a few seconds. *Looks official.* He ran a finger under the lip and pulled out a single sheet of white paper. The blood drained from his face when he read the message.

Major Wu is going to die a horrible death. Signed with the initials P.T.

"P.T.? That's Princeton Taylor. He's kidnapped Joan."

Matt didn't expect this. He thought the MPs would arrest her on some trumped-up charge. *How naïve. We're dealing with a psychopath.*

Horrible images flashed through his mind. Joan gagged and tied up in some moldy basement of a vacant house. Then he saw her tied naked against a tree in the woods, left for the ants and the wild animals to strip pieces of flesh from her body. Then he saw her hands and feet bound by duct tape, in the trunk of a car. He shook his head. *I've been reading too many Stephen King novels.*

He left his office, and in the corridor, he pulled out the FBI cell phone from his pocket to call Chris Cousins. While waiting for him to answer, he thought about how his relationship with Joan had improved. How much he loved her, more than ever.

When Chris answered, Matt said, "Taylor's kidnapped Joan."

"When?"

"Sometime between one and one-thirty. She went to lunch with Jagger but left the club alone to run an errand to the post office. A courier delivered a note to me from Taylor, informing me that she was going to die a horrible death."

"I now know why Taylor was saving you," said Chris. "He's galvanizing you to come after her. He'll secrete her in the warehouse, knowing you'll try to save her." He paused for a few seconds. "He wants you both together when he releases Omega Bytes on al-Qaeda."

Matt thought about what Joan had told him: General Taylor became enraged when she gave him the letter, resigning her commission. He shouted at her, calling her an ingrate and a disgrace to the military for siding with a civilian. Taylor denied her request and threw the sheet in her face. She stormed out of his office, hating him more.

"Chris, what are we going to do?" said Matt.

"Just sit tight." Then he hung up.

Matt dialed the number for his Stanford friend, Dr. Fabor Keyes.

"Sir, this is Matt."

"What's wrong? You sound distressed."

"General Taylor's gone crazy. He's going to release a bioweapon against al-Qaeda in Newark."

Matt could hear Keyes breathing hard into the phone.

"I thought about going to Dr. Rutherford for help but then remembered you were the Science Advisor to the last President."

"It's been too long," said Keyes. "I'm out of the Washington coterie, and haven't kept in touch with them."

"I really need your help, Fabor. Taylor's kidnapped my friend, Joan Wu, and I'm afraid for her."

"I'm sorry, Matt. I've got a pressing problem here. Can't get involved." Then he paused, apparently searching his mind for a name. "David would be your best bet; he has many friends in Washington, especially the mighty powerful Senator Fellows."

"Thank you," said Matt, feeling disappointed in Keyes. He sensed something strange about him. Usually, he was willing and able to help him.

"You're not thinking about doing anything stupid—are you, Matt?"

"Taylor wants us both dead," said Matt. "That's why he kidnapped Joan. He knows I'll come after her."

CHAPTER FIFTY-FOUR

Matt hurried to the red elevators and rode one down to the first floor. When the doors opened, he stepped into the corridor and looked around. He recognized the same medicinal odor coming from the manufacturing area in the back. He saw no one he knew, so he slipped into the CEO's office across the hall.

Dr. David Rutherford III, President and CEO of DnaTech, an internationally known geneticist, educated at Harvard, had received the Nobel Prize in Human Gene Therapy. Matt remembered his mesmerizing talks at Stanford. The research faculty mentioned Rutherford's name more than any other during Matt's graduate school days at University of Chicago.

Matt found Molly Logan at her desk when he entered the office. That's the name he read on the nameplate. He saw her a few times in the parking lot, but they never spoke.

"I'm Matt Brenner, Molly. I work on six. Would it be possible for me to see Dr. Rutherford?"

"Oh, I know who you are, Dr. Brenner," she said.

Matt's eyes widen, and then he smiled at her.

"Don't look so surprised," she said. "We know everyone in the building. That's how Dr. Rutherford works."

"I'm impressed."

Molly stood and came from behind her desk—a short, middle-aged lady, with a slender body and light brown hair tinted with a faint touch of red. She wore sexy-looking plastic rim glasses that could qualify her as the cat lady. She had a pleasant smile. "Let's see if he'll see you, Dr. Brenner," she said, moving to the adjoining office, and disappeared.

Matt regarded the bright rectangular room furnished with red leather side-arm chairs lined against the dark-paneled walls. On square tables in each corner stood lamps with *National Geographic*, *The New Yorker*, and *Newsweek* magazines arranged in an organized way below them. Pictures of the DnaTech building, grounds, manufacturing areas and some laboratories hung on the walls, and a light-blue carpet brightened the room. Matt's eyes widened when the door opened and Dr. Rutherford appeared. He hadn't expected the CEO to come out and greet him.

"Please come in, Dr. Brenner," he said, smiling. "Haven't seen you since my Stanford visits. That was a few years ago."

"Thanks for seeing me, Dr. Rutherford," said Matt. He followed the CEO into the large office, passing a long conference table with red leather chairs. He saw his face reflected in the surface of the conference table.

"Have a seat," Rutherford said, pointing to the leather chairs in front of his desk, "I'll be with you in a minute."

Matt adjusted his sport coat as he sank into one of the chairs. Rutherford moved some papers to one side of his executive desk, and then sat in a high-backed swivel chair. A painting of the DnaTech building hung in a wide gold frame on the wall behind his desk and over a credenza. Matt scanned the gold-framed pictures on the credenza of Rutherford's family: four daughters, a son, and twelve grandchildren. He counted them as he waited for the CEO to look up. His desk was neat, just what Matt had expected from a man who dressed in a nine-hundred-dollar blue business suit and a one-hundred-dollar silk tie. Tall and healthy looking, Rutherford played tennis—the pictures gave it away—and his tan proved it. He was young looking for someone in his late sixties. Matt smiled, thinking that he must have had a politician for a mentor. He certainly looked the part.

"Now, what can I do for you?" said Rutherford, closing a folder and clasping his hands together.

"I don't know where to begin," said Matt, sitting up straight. "Sir, no one knows I'm here."

"I understand," said Rutherford. "Since I didn't hear from Colonel Jagger's office about your visit, I figured you're here on a mission of your own."

Matt couldn't help but think that Rutherford had psychic powers. "Yes, sir. Thanks for seeing me."

"Now, your mission?"

Matt knew Rutherford was a man who went directly to the point and expected others to do the same.

"We have a situation in the biodefense center."

Rutherford frowned. "How serious?"

"Beyond comprehension."

"What might that be?"

"A biological weapon."

Matt could see his eyes narrow. "What is the biological?"

"A genetically altered killer virus that devours flesh, leaving bones and hair in a gelatinous mass." A pause while Matt locked on Rutherford's gaze. "It's a slatewiper, sir."

Rutherford blinked with surprise. "I have never heard of a virus that can dissolve a body."

"Neither had I. Dr. Max Tandenbaum engineered it from two other viruses. Gene swapping."

Matt told Rutherford about Project Game Point. Then he introduced him to the Omega Bytes computer.

Rutherford said, "You mean a biological virus that can be released from a computer?"

"Yes."

"Viruses are labile. How is his virus kept stable?"

"Lyophilization," said Matt.

"And the board heats the well in the chip and the moisture revitalizes the virus," said Rutherford.

"Yes."

A pause while Rutherford fell into deep thought. Seconds later, he said, "I take it that General Taylor has some dreadful plan involving this virus, and that's why you are here?"

Matt nodded. "He plans on releasing it in Newark on al-Qaeda. They're using a warehouse as an import-export business to store their weapons, to recruit, and to have training sessions."

Rutherford's facial muscles tightened.

"The FBI has learned the general's going to release the virus a week from Friday."

"Ten days from now," added Rutherford, looking at the calendar on his desk.

Matt watched Rutherford while he wrote something on the calendar. Then he said, "I don't know how to say this, sir."

"Go ahead."

"The general's crazy as hell. If he releases that virus, millions of innocent people will die. We have antidote, but not enough. This virus travels fast." He reached into his pocket. "I got this note from the general today," said Matt, rising from his chair to hand it to Rutherford.

Rutherford's eyes glanced over the note.

"I thought... maybe..." Matt stopped.

"You thought?" said Rutherford, folding the note and handing it back to Matt who returned to his chair.

"I thought this misuse of the Biodefense Center by the general would be a good reason for you to remove the Center from DnaTech."

The tall man's brow furrowed. "And how would I do that?"

"I understand you have powerful friends in Washington."

He smiled. "You have done your homework."

"Yes, sir. I've done some checking."

Rutherford got up, went to the window, and stared out into a garden that was almost bare. Matt had asked Joan about the garden under the CEO's window. She explained that Rutherford loved flowers, and he designed the garden in memory of his wife, who died after forty years of marriage. Rutherford rubbed his lower lip and stood there gazing out the window.

Matt wondered if Rutherford received some kind of inspiration from the garden. The CEO returned to his chair and gazed at Matt for a few seconds, then said, "I believe General Taylor has given me enough ammunition to investigate this more thoroughly."

"Thank you, sir."

"What's your plan?" asked Rutherford.

"With the help of the FBI and local authorities, I'm going to Newark to dismantle the computer."

"And what about the major?"

Matt moved forward in his chair. "I love her," he said with passion in his voice. "I hope to get her out of there alive."

"And General Taylor?" asked Rutherford.

"I don't know, sir. My main concern is the major and the people of Newark. They come first."

"Very noble. I wish you the best," said Rutherford as he rose, buttoned his suit coat, and came from behind his desk.

Matt stood, and said, "I figure the FBI can handle General Taylor."

With a hand extended, Rutherford said, "Let's get the bastard, Dr. Brenner."

CHAPTER FIFTY-FIVE

Matt left Rutherford's office pleased with himself. His plan for Taylor's demise had begun. When he entered his office, he heard his cell phone and picked it up.

"Yes, Chris."

"I have some news—"

"Me first," Matt said, cutting him off. "Dr. Rutherford feels the time is right to remove the Army from this place."

"That is good news," said Chris.

"Whatta you mean, *good*? It's great."

"I have some not-so-good news."

"I'm afraid to ask. What is it?"

"We spotted Taylor."

"The not-so-good news is that you didn't get him?"

"Afraid not."

"What about Joan?"

"Still haven't found her."

"Where could he have her?"

"He's probably concealed her in the warehouse." He paused. "Got some bad news."

Matt sighed. "Stop playing with me!"

"Al-Qaeda has bumped up their training session to this Friday."

Matt slammed his fist on the desk. "That only gives us two days."

"I'm afraid so."

"Okay, okay," said Matt. "You and Taylor win. Round up all your people and do whatever you have to do, 'cause I'm going in Friday night to get her and to dismantle the Omega Bytes computer."

"We'll go in with you," said Chris.

Matt bolted from his chair. "No! Hell no! Just me. Taylor'll set off Omega Bytes if he sees FBI."

"But you'll need cover. I don't know…"

"Can't risk it. I'm doing this alone. And that's final."

"Okay, okay. It's doable." Matt envisioned Chris holding up his hands in a gesture of submission as they talked. "You're right. One person might pull it off," said Chris.

"That's the way it's going to be," said Matt. "How do I get there?"

"Be at the helipad behind DnaTech in the morning at six o'clock. And don't forget the antidote."

CHAPTER FIFTY-SIX

Dr. David Rutherford's plane had landed at the Ronald Reagan National Airport at five in the afternoon. While he had been to Washington, DC many times, he never liked the hustling of people and bustling of traffic. World traveler David Rutherford never liked airports.

The baggage area appeared in total chaos. He pushed his way through the throng of travelers to search for his luggage. Handlers sorted the luggage according to flight numbers, then threw the bags out to the people from the inoperable carousels. He waved for a porter. Children stepped on his shoes as they pushed him aside. *Why in the hell don't parents keep watch over their children?* Rutherford caught sight of his limo driver walking through the entrance and heading his way. *Thank God!*

As they left the terminal, cars, taxis, shuttle buses and limos moved through the four-lane street in front of the entrance. Horns blew at them, irate drivers screamed at one another. Travelers rushed across the street with their luggage in hand or they pushed little two-wheelers. Cabbies screamed at cars that pulled in front of them, giving them the finger, while the intruders replied with an equally unkind gesture. Rutherford's limo driver led the way across the street, carrying the CEO's briefcase while Rutherford followed the porter pushing the cart with his luggage.

———◆———

The next morning, Rutherford entered the Senate Capitol Building and caught a glimpse of Senator Ted Kennedy as he entered an office with his aides. Rutherford turned and went to Senator Fellow's office.

The waiting-room door flew open, and a man in his early thirties, dressed in a brown suit and green tie, popped out. They nodded at each other, and Rutherford stepped inside the door.

The room smelled of Aramis cologne. In the back was a man reading a magazine and a woman working the keyboard on her laptop. Two brown leather chairs with an end table and lamp against one wall matched the set at the opposite wall. A handsome man in his mid-thirties, thin, wearing a light blue suit, stood at the desk ahead of Rutherford talking to the secretary. He figured the man for a lobbyist. The man turned and left.

Ms. Knopp smiled, then said, "Good to see you again, Dr. Rutherford."

"Thank you, Ms. Knopp," he said. "I'm here for my nine o'clock."

"Yes, of course, sir," she said, glancing at the appointment book. She rose and came from behind her desk. "I'll let the Senator know you're here." Rutherford regarded Knopp: plump, in her early fifties, with some gray strands in her short black hair. She wore wide silver-rimmed eyeglasses held at the sides by black- and gold-braided strings that looped in front of her shoulders against a white blouse.

She reappeared from the office to his left. "The Senator will see you now, Dr. Rutherford." The door behind her sprang open and a tall, gray-haired man in a light tan suit and solid blue tie appeared.

"David, good to see you again. Come in."

"Thanks, Warren. Good of you to see me on short notice."

"Anytime, David. You know that."

A stalwart Republican and a prisoner of war in Vietnam for two years, Warren Fellows had collected mementos over the last thirty years that were on display around his office. Photographs of presidents, the Capitol and political memorabilia hung on the walls. Fellows had mentioned to Rutherford on several occasions how proud he was of his roots and his country. On the credenza were Warren's Silver Star and Purple Heart earned in Vietnam, next to a group picture of Fellows' family—wife and two sons. The Senator stood proud in the picture. Rutherford recognized the senator's parents—successful cattle farmers in Montana.

Fellows looked healthy and trim and didn't smoke or drink. He must still do his 100 pushups in the morning, thought Rutherford, a discipline Fellows told him he started when he was a prisoner in Vietnam.

"Let's sit over there, David," the Senator said, pointing in the direction of a coffee table separating two large cushioned chairs facing the couch.

Rutherford chose one of the chairs.

"How about something to drink?"

"Black coffee," said Rutherford.

Fellows returned with a cup of coffee and a can of caffeine-free Diet Coke.

Rutherford had picked up two of Fellows' publications from the coffee table and glanced through them while waiting for his coffee.

"Those are my committee's publications on the mistreatment of our veterans by the Department of Defense," he said as he handed Rutherford the cup, then eased into the other chair.

Fellows was chairman of the Senate Committee investigating the Defense Department. "The American people would be shocked if they knew all the facts in those books," he said, pointing to them.

"I remember your quote in *Newsweek*," said Rutherford.

"I don't mind telling you," said Fellows, positioning himself on the edge of his chair. "For fifty years, the DoD has secretly exposed our military to dangerous substances." He shook his head. "And civilians, I might add."

Rutherford took a sip of his coffee and reflected on his involvement in numerous clinical trials as principal investigator. He and his coworkers had to explain the test protocol to the volunteers as they signed release forms.

"I'm mad as hell at the DoD," said Fellows. "Some are arrogant bastards. Excuse my French." He took a sip of his soft drink and set it on the coffee table. "Sorry, David," said the senator. "I didn't mean to get on that. But it riles me."

"I understand."

"Now tell me, how can I help you?"

"Have you ever heard of an Army General by the name of Princeton Taylor?"

Fellows reeled with wide eyes. "Taylor?" Fellows leaned in to Rutherford. "He's the one that supervised those DoD experiments." He grabbed his empty soft drink can, rose, and took it to the counter. He paced the floor for a few seconds, then said, "Taylor's been before my committee several times. Talk about arrogance. I think he's a psycho case."

"I'm afraid he's unbalanced," said Rutherford.

Fellows returned to his chair. "Did you ever hear of the Project Game Point?" he asked, gazing into Rutherford's eyes.

"A molecular biologist at my company told me about it."

"In Vietnam, Taylor used twelve of our men in an experiment without permission and lied to them. Eleven died."

"That's why I'm here, Warren."

"If it has anything to do with Taylor, I'm your man."

Rutherford smiled, knowing with Fellows in his corner, he could break his agreement with the Pentagon.

"The last time we talked, Warren, I mentioned my agreement with the Army. We needed their infusion of funds to survive the biotech competition. But I'm outraged at what they have done in the Center. They lied to me."

"What specifically has he done?"

"Taylor's developed a genetically altered biological that can be released from a computer."

"A computer?"

"A biocomputer. One with a live virus in its microchip." A pause. "And Taylor plans to release it in Newark in a few days against a group of al-Qaeda."

Fellows looked at the ceiling for a few seconds, then turned to Rutherford. "Are you saying this lunatic is actually going to release a virus in an American city?"

"That's exactly what I'm saying. And he knows it will kill millions of Americans, but he doesn't give a damn."

"We'll have to see about that," said Fellows.

"This Dr. Brenner I mentioned, he's tormented by a potential holocaust. He sought my help and you were the first one I thought of."

Fellows jumped up. "Taylor must be stopped now."

"The FBI and Dr. Brenner are in Newark as we speak," said Rutherford.

Fellows nodded, went to his desk, and picked up the telephone. "This is Senator Fellows. I need to meet with the Secretary. It's urgent." A pause. "Thank you." He turned and looked at Rutherford. "The Defense Secretary will see me in one hour."

Rutherford stood. "Thank you, Warren."

"It's time Taylor is put away for good, and the Army's Biodefense Center is dismantled," said Fellows.

CHAPTER FIFTY-SEVEN

The sun peeped over the horizon that Thursday morning, and the cool air felt refreshing as it brushed over Matt's face. He placed his gear at the helicopter pad behind DnaTech Pharmaceuticals and waited for his ride. In the distance, the whop... whop... whop of its rotor announced the arrival of a chopper, and a few seconds later an Air Force chopper skimmed the trees, descending to the pad like a vulture about to pounce its prey. The rotary blades created a whirlwind of dust like a tornado around the pad, prompting Matt to cover his eyes until the chopper set down. He bent forward, rushed to the chopper, threw his gear onboard, jumped in, and placed a small satchel on his lap. The big bird took off as quickly as it landed.

When the chopper set down at Powell Air Force Base, thirty miles on the Illinois side of the Mississippi River, Matt grabbed his gear, opened the door and moved out carefully, ducking under the rotating blades. He stood by the gate looking for his contact. He had no idea who that would be. In the distance, a jeep approached at a high rate of speed. The driver motioned to Matt.

"Dr. Brenner?"

"Yes."

"Jump in."

He threw his gear in the back and hopped in the front with the satchel, then the driver sped away. Coming to a stop at the other end of the base, close to an Air Force C-141 Starlifter with its engines roaring, the driver said, "That's your ride."

Matt jumped out, grabbed his gear, and ran to the plane. A female sergeant standing in the doorway called out his name. Jet engines blasted a path of air that fluttered his pant legs like flags in a March wind.

He lowered his head to keep the dust out of his eyes as he ran to the plane. The smell of jet fuel took his breath. He threw in his duffle bag and jumped in. The sergeant thrust a parachute into his gut.

"Find a place to sit," she said, "and be quick about it." The door slammed shut behind him. He looked around inside the huge belly of the plane. Air Force officers sat on metal benches with their backs against the walls, using their parachutes as seat cushions. No one looked his way; they were too busy talking.

Matt dodged massive military equipment to make his way to the back of the plane, dragging the duffel bag and holding on to the leather satchel. He was the only civilian. During the flight no one spoke to him, but he overheard the officers talking about terrorist cells in the Middle East.

As the C-141 touched down at an East Coast Air Force base, Matt saw a C-5 Galaxy transport on a runway being loaded with vehicles and Army personnel. The C-141 taxied on a parallel runway two runways from the other transports. Matt took his time deplaning, watching as the officers boarded jeeps. Once they moved away from the jet, he looked around for the sergeant. She had disappeared. Matt waited. He looked around again, but saw only the officers heading to the big transports. *I'm glad I'm a civilian.* He placed a handkerchief over his nose and mouth to barricade the biting smell of jet fuel.

Where are those agents? He started to cough. He saw another jeep speeding toward him with a female Air Force person and a man in a trench coat sitting in the passenger side. The civilian yelled out Matt's name above the noise of the jet engines. Matt waved, picked up his gear, ran to the vehicle, threw in the canvass bag, held on to the satchel, and jumped in. They sped away, coming to a stop six hundred yards from his pickup point. The driver pulled next to a black sedan parked on the side of the Command Headquarters building. Matt saw the government plates and began to relax. The back door of the sedan opened and a man in a black suit emerged. He grabbed Matt's gear, but Matt held on to the satchel and slid in next to another agent. The agent who took his gear stored it in the trunk, then slid in next to Matt and slammed the door. As they drove away, Matt looked at the back of the person seated on the passenger's side and sighed. He leaned forward and handed the satchel to Special Agent Chris Cousins.

CHAPTER FIFTY-EIGHT

They arrived in Newark before sunset and circled al-Qaeda headquarters in an abandoned chemical warehouse on the edge of town near the river. It covered an area equivalent to half a city block with a parking area that surrounded the warehouse like a sea around an island. It could accommodate over a hundred cars. They drove on to the command post across the street and several buildings down from the warehouse. The command center occupied a vacant building, which had housed an auto repair and muffler shop, with five apartment units upstairs. FBI surveillance equipment on the top floor had been in place for weeks, following al-Qaeda movements. Chris then had the driver take them to their motel. After a meal they settled in their rooms.

"We're sharing a room?" said Matt.

"Cutting costs."

"Or maybe you don't trust me?" said Matt.

Chris smiled. "That too."

"Take me to the motel Taylor stayed at."

"She's not in there, Matt," said Chris. "They're gone."

"I'd feel better if I could just see the place."

Traffic was heavy, and Matt watched the road as Chris drove the black sedan. Fifteen minutes later, they parked at the curb in front of the Regency Motel, motor running, lights off.

"Which room?" asked Matt.

"Number 125 down on the end by the fenced-in pool."

"Did they check out?"

"I'm telling you, she's not in there. And they didn't check out," said Chris. "They registered as David Allen and Bill Winthrop."

"Where did they come up with those names?"

Chris shrugged. "Who knows?"

"Pull down there by the pool," said Matt, gesturing. "I want to get a closer look."

"If it'll make you happy. But we need to get back. Got a big day tomorrow."

"I just want to look at the place for a few minutes. That's all."

Chris moved the sedan toward the pool with the lights off and pulled into a parking place parallel to the fence. The heated pool closed at nine, and it was half-past the hour. No one was around.

"Room 125 is dark," said Matt.

"They're gone."

"Or in hiding. Why didn't you throw a net around this place and cart them off?"

"So, you're telling me how to do my job?"

"You told me you couldn't arrest Taylor because he hadn't done anything. You could have gotten him on kidnapping charges."

"Do you want Taylor to kill her? He'll do just that if he thinks we're closing in on him. What does he have to lose?"

Matt knew Chris was right. Was he getting cold feet about tomorrow? Is that why he wanted Chris to find her? So he wouldn't have to go in the warehouse. Then he thought about Jesus in Gethsemane. *Even he got cold feet. I can't just sit here.* He rammed his shoulder against the passenger door and propelled out of the car.

"Hold it, where do you think you're going?" said Chris, striking the door with his shoulder. He chased after Matt. "What the hell are you doing?"

Matt darted around the front of the car and sprinted around the fence and onto the walkway, staying close to the building, under the overhang, to shield him from the parking lot lights. He grabbed the doorknob of room 125, but before he could hit the door with his shoulder, an arm hooked his neck and threw him to the ground. His head bounced on the pavement, knocking him out.

Back in their motel, Chris dabbed a piece of gauze with antiseptic and pressed it on Matt's head.

"Ouch!" Matt shouted, lying on the bed.

"Hold still for Chrissake," said Chris.

"Where am I?"

"Back at the room. That was a stupid thing you did."

"What happened?"

"Two DIA agents pounced on your ass, and you hit your head on the pavement. Good thing I got there with my guys."

"You had agents following us?"

"Couldn't take any chances," said Chris, scowling at Matt. "You could have gotten Joan killed. I hope you realize that."

Matt didn't respond.

"Remember, Taylor's not stable, and we don't know what will set him off."

"What were the DIA agents doing there?"

"Taylor didn't tell them to report in," said Chris, "so they didn't know he wasn't coming back."

"Maybe by now Taylor's got Joan in the warehouse."

"My men didn't see them go in. But that's a possibility."

"Chris?"

"Yes," he said, climbing into bed.

"I'm sorry. I just couldn't help it. When I thought she might be tied up in that room, I lost it."

"Try and get some sleep. Tomorrow's a big day."

"Have you taken the measures we talked about?" said Matt.

"The fire trucks and hand sprayers have been filled with the bleach solution. Everything's ready. Get some sleep."

CHAPTER FIFTY-NINE

Besides having a horrible night, this new day would become the longest day of Matt's life. He tried to build up his confidence knowing that the FBI had scoured the city looking for Joan, which meant she had to be in the warehouse, alive. Still, he feared he might not be able to save her in time.

Matt had slipped into his dark biohazard suit, but decided he'd wait to put on the helmet until he entered the warehouse. He hooked a silenced 9mm Glock and a metal case containing small tools to his belt, spreading them apart to hang from each side of his hips, along with two doses of antidote.

"Just about ready," said Chris Cousins as he jumped up and down to get comfortable in his biohazard suit. "Don't forget Joan's suit."

"I won't." Matt picked up the extra biohazard suit and moved to the door. "Let's go." They descended a flight of stairs to the first floor with their plastic helmets in their hands and made it to a platform.

FBI antiterrorist teams, biological weapons experts, fireman, and local authorities in dark biohazard gear moved around the platform.

"Let me have your attention, please," Chris called out as he and Matt ascended the platform.

"Okay everyone. It's time. Dr. Brenner's going into the warehouse to find Major Wu and to dismantle the computer. You'll stand ready outside the warehouse. Those of you with hand sprayers, are you ready?"

"WE'RE READY, SIR!"

"Antiterrorism personnel. Are you ready?"

"READY, SIR!"

"Agents, fireman, biological weapons experts. Are you ready?"

"YES, SIR! WE'RE READY, SIR! LET'S GET 'EM!"

"Okay. You know the dangers we're facing. The fire trucks will move into place once Dr. Brenner moves in. Additional medical personnel are standing by in the city and will be called in if needed. Dr. Brenner has thirty minutes to find Major Wu and dismantle the computer. In the event he doesn't, we'll go in on my command. Wait for my signal. Any questions?"

No one raised a hand or called out to him.

Chris glanced at Matt. "Dr. Brenner has something to say."

Matt paused to look out at the army of faces. *Please God, don't let me fail.* "Let me assure you I don't plan to fail," said Matt. "Let's kick ass." He stepped down from the platform and moved to the door.

The FBI lookouts had reported that the way was clear. Like waves of black beetles, the teams moved through the shadows toward the windowless warehouse. Matt looked at his watch. Eight-fifty. Ten minutes before he would go in. The lead FBI agents watched for late al-Qaeda arrivals.

"So far, so good," said Chris to Matt as everyone moved toward the entrance of the warehouse.

Firefighters' pump trucks filled with bleach solutions moved into place, waiting for the word to spray foam over the entire building. Human decontamination trucks moved into the parking lot. Teams of firefighters with hand sprayers filled with bleach solutions stood ready to spray down the inside of the building and every person in there, dead or alive. Hundreds of FBI antiterrorism and rescue teams dressed in black biohazard suits, holding weapons in the air, stood ready.

Matt opened the steel door and eased inside with Joan's biohazard suit, which weighed him down some. His heart raced, and his ears popped. He felt claustrophobic in the suit, so he took a deep breath to take his mind off of it. He blinked to adjust to the dim light provided by a single light bulb across the room, suspended from the ceiling by a thin wire, which did little to illuminate the large area.

"Where are you, Joan?" he said to himself as he moved deeper into the building.

A cacophony of sounds came from behind a partially opened steel door that slid on a track. A stream of light came from the narrow opening, streaking the floor at an angle. He could see the dust mites floating in the light as he moved to the edge of the door and peeked into the big hall. About one hundred Middle Eastern men and women in casual clothes jumped up and down to the cadence of their leader's praise to Allah.

Matt moved away from the door toward the center of the spacious room, looking the place over. Stairs in the back led up to a landing thirty feet above his head. He wondered if Omega Bytes could be up there. To his left were three doors, and some old workbenches to his right, and under the stairs, an abandoned chemistry lab.

Instinctively, he moved to the first door and placed Joan's biohazard suit on the floor. His heart pounded as he turned the knob. "Shit! It's locked." He tapped several times on the door and whispered, "Joan... Joan this is Matt." No answer. Suddenly, he jerked around.

One of the terrorists had moved the big door aside and went to one of the benches. Matt held his breath as he stood in a shadow against the door. The man glanced in his direction. Matt's heart beat against his rib cage and perspiration popped out on his forehead. The man removed something from the bench, then stood for a few seconds looking toward Matt, before he went back into the big hall and slid the big door close.

Matt released his breath and moved to the second door. He tapped on it and called out Joan's name in a whisper. Nothing. He moved to the third door. He tapped on it. He heard a muffled cry. Matt reached for the small box on his belt. Removing a small tool from it, he fumbled with the lock; his hands shook. He tried again. A click. He turned the knob. The door opened. He entered, closed it behind him, and flipped on the light. Joan sat on the concrete floor next to a small sink with her back against the wall and her knees up under her chin. She had her face resting on her knees, moaning.

"Thank God," he said.

She hitched her head when the light flashed on. She moaned louder when she saw him. Her hands were tied behind her back, and her feet were tied at the ankles. The smell of cleaning liquids saturated the closet. A large trash barrel partially shielded her, but Matt knocked it to one side, jerked the duct tape and gag from Joan's mouth, then untied her feet and hands.

"I knew you'd come," she said. "Thank God!"

He pulled her up and grabbed her in his arms.

"You're shaking," she said.

"Hell yes! I was scared to death. How about you, you okay?"

She steadied herself. "Give me a few seconds."

"We gotta hurry," said Matt. He turned to open the door. He went for her biohazard suit. "Put this on."

"Taylor and Ash are upstairs," said Joan as she slipped into the biohazard suit. "Omega Bytes is down here somewhere in a box with another computer. They hadn't taken them up to the office yet."

Matt pulled her along toward the boxes.

She stopped and pointed to a stack of boxes in the center of the room. "THERE THEY ARE," she shouted through her plastic faceplate.

CHAPTER SIXTY

Taylor and Ash stood in the dimmed light on the second floor landing, near a metal balustrade, watching the terrorists trickle into the big hall. Once they had closed the steel door, Taylor told Ash to watch for Brenner while he went into the small office.

"I'll keep an eye out."

Minutes later, Ash cried out, "Son of a bitch." He rushed into the office.

"Brenner's freed the major, and they're breaking into the boxes."

Taylor rushed to the railing.

"Hello, Brenner. You took my bait. I've got something for you two."

Taylor dashed into the office with Ash in his wake.

"Release the virus now, General! Release it!"

"What good would that do?" screamed Taylor. "They're in biohazard suits."

Ash knocked him to one side, grabbed the remote from the desk, and darted out. Taylor grabbed a long piece of heavy metal pipe leaning against the door, sprinted after Ash, and bludgeoned him to death.

"I'll say when it's time."

Taylor picked up the remote and stood by the railing. Matt and Joan were tearing into boxes.

He smiled.

CHAPTER SIXTY-ONE

Matt grabbed the top box.

"THAT'S NOT IT," Joan said.

He grabbed the box underneath and worked off the top with some difficulty because of the rubber gloves he wore. He toppled the box on its side, crushed in the top, while Joan stood by with a flashlight.

"THIS IS NOT IT." He tore into another box. Chemicals. He could hear his heart pounding in his ears.

"WHERE IN THE HELL IS IT?" he shouted.

"IT'S GOT TO BE HERE," she shouted. "I SAW TAYLOR'S MEN BRING THEM IN."

Joan struggled with her helmet.

Thinking she was about to remove it, Matt shouted, "FOR CHRISSAKE—DON'T! THAT'S WHAT HE WANTS." *The light is so damn dim. Where did he put it?*

He bumped into several large boxes outside an old chemistry lab, then tore into them like a madman. Small metal cylinders.

"THESE ARE FILLED WITH NERVE GAS." He looked toward the large steel door and said, "YOU SCUMBAGS."

CHAPTER SIXTY-TWO

Taylor charged down the stairs. At the bottom of the steps, he grabbed a round metal gas tank that came up to his hips, standing outside the old chemistry lab.

———◆———

Joan knelt next to Matt, who went to his knees to yank off the top of the last box.

"HERE IT IS," shouted Matt. He ripped off the top of the computer.

"You traitors!" shouted Taylor, charging at them with a crazed look, holding the metal tank high above his head. Within a few feet, Taylor hurled it, but missed them. It crashed into the Omega Bytes computer, splitting it open.

Startled, Matt swung around, knocking Joan to the floor, causing her helmet to flip off. Matt's Glock bounced on the floor.

Matt lunged at Taylor. During the struggle, the general yanked off Matt's helmet and tore his suit, knocking him to his knees. Taylor pulled out the remote from his pocket and shouted, "I have something for you two."

Matt dove for the computer. Joan aimed the Glock at Taylor and got off two rounds, hitting him in the stomach. As Taylor fell backwards, he released the virus, shouting, "Too late. Both of you are dead meat."

Matt bolted over to Joan. "I couldn't dismantle it." He pulled the antidotes from his side and administered it to her and then to himself.

CHAPTER SIXTY-THREE

FBI antiterrorism teams raced into the warehouse followed by firefighters with hand sprayers. Spreading throughout the warehouse and up the stairs, they formed a huge web. Firefighters began spraying every inch of the building and every dead person.

The antiterrorist teams had found Taylor with his flesh gone, only his skeleton in a gooey mass, and the al-Qaeda insurgents were bleeding out. An hour later the al-Qaeda remains were sprayed, bagged, and then the bags were sprayed.

EMT personnel assisted Matt and Joan out of the warehouse.

Strobe lights flashed and blinding floodlights turned night into day. Bleach foam covered the building, dripping down the sides and forming puddles on the ground. Dozens of Newark police and FBI vehicles filled the parking lot and fire trucks surrounded the building. Hundreds of antiterrorism personnel, wearing black biohazard suits, scurried on the grounds.

Matt and Joan were put through the decontamination truck and then into quarantine as a safety measure.

Matt turned to Joan and studied her face as they sat in quarantine. He looked deep into her brown eyes. She smiled. Her beauty sent sparks over his skin. He thought about all he had gone through since her kidnapping and knew he'd do it all again for her. Finally, he said, "I was really scared going in there. I didn't think I'd find you in time, but I kept telling myself that I would. The moment impacted me. I realized, without you, I wouldn't have a life."

She smiled and squeezed his hand.

"When I found you tied up in that closet with your knees up in your chest, my heart ached, but then I realized how lucky I was to find you."

She hugged him and held him for several minutes. Matt eased backwards and looked at her. Tears welled up in her eyes.

"I love you, Matt," she said. She took a deep breath. "I had always thought of myself as an independent person, but when Richard died, I had to lean on someone. Kenny was there for me. Then you came to Fort Detrick, and I started to live again." She paused to wipe her tears. "I fell in love with you, but I allowed Kenny to put a wedge between us." She looked into Matt's gaze, and said, "Forgive me?"

"Of course."

CHAPTER SIXTY-FOUR

Chris waited for Matt and Joan as they were released from quarantine.

"You guys okay? You look a little pale."

Matt waved the comment off. "We're great."

They followed Chris to his sedan where he opened the back door on the driver's side.

"Wait inside, I won't be long," he said. He moved to the front of the car and called out to one of his agents in the other car.

"They found Captain Ash's body upstairs," said Matt.

"I heard," she said. "I'm glad it's all over."

He nodded. "Now that Jack's murderers are dead."

Matt glanced at Chris who was talking to two of his men. When Matt turned back to Joan, he frowned.

"What's wrong? You seem pensive."

"I resigned my commission. I went to the post office to mail it to General Whitehead. That's when they abducted me. Thank God I got it mailed."

"I'm glad," said Matt. "That fits into my plans."

Her brow contracted. "What plans?"

"Our wedding plans." Then he winked.

Her hand went to her chest. "Are you asking me to marry you?"

"I think so," he said in a teasing way.

She grabbed his neck, pulled him to her, and kissed him. Then she said, "I accept."

Chris opened the car door, slipped in behind the wheel, turned and glanced over his shoulder.

"Mors is still at large. We've got a few leads. It's just a matter of time."

Chris started the car and backed out of the parking lot. "You'll be glad to know that the Army is moving out of DnaTech as we speak."

"Great! I knew Dr. Rutherford would come through," said Matt.

"He got to Senator Fellows," said Chris.

The sedan lunged as Chris depressed the accelerator and moved into the traffic.

"Matt? You remember your friend Police Chief Brewer?"

"My friend? You got to be kidding."

"He committed suicide."

"That's convenient," said Matt.

"Our investigation turned up something quite interesting. He and Taylor had a symbiotic relationship. The Chief wanted the homeless out of his city, and the general made the problem go away. The M.E. squealed on them. He also implicated one of Chief Brewer's officers. Turns out the mayor wasn't involved in any of this."

"What about Devlin?" asked Matt.

"The agent you saw in the police station caught that officer implicated by the M.E. The officer confessed that the chief had him kill Devlin as a favor to the general for getting rid of their homeless problem."

"So, Taylor did want Devlin out of the way," said Matt.

Chris nodded. "Because he was snooping around and getting dangerously close to exposing Taylor."

"Good work," said Matt.

"What are you guys going to do now?" asked Chris.

"We're going on our honeymoon, and after a couple of months we may go back to USAMRIID."

Chris hitched his head around. His eyebrows shot up.

"Oh, I guess congratulations are in order."

CHAPTER SIXTY-FIVE

Two months later, Matt and Joan returned to DnaTech to gather their books and personal items from their offices, to meet with Dr. Rutherford. They were surprised not to see the Army guards as they approached the southwest entrance. The shack and fence were gone. No gates. Matt drove straight through and parked next to the building. They went through the southwest entrance to the red elevators, which now were silver. The doors opened, and they stepped in.

"Look at this," said Matt. "Buttons for every floor." He punched the one for six, and when the doors slid opened, they found themselves in a corridor.

"The guards are gone," said Matt, looking around. "No more security."

"And the walls? Even the blue door is gone," said Joan. "It's all open."

They could see down an aisle made from piles of doors, metal frames and plasterboards stacked against new walls. They moved with caution through the aisle so not to catch their clothes on the sharp edges and dodged workers carrying tools and materials into the new rooms. The dust was unbearable. They covered their mouths and noses with their hands, and looked into unfinished laboratories. The entire floor seemed strange to them. The dust cleared and Joan said, "This is a little eerie."

"I think this is where my lab was," said Matt.

"This seems about right."

As they turned to head back to the elevators, a security guard approached them and asked if he could help them.

Matt introduced himself and then Joan. "We were wondering

what happened to our things."

"We packed everything and put it in storage," said the guard.

Joan looked at her watch and then at Matt, "About time to meet with Rutherford."

"I'll look for your boxes, take them to the southwest entrance, and wait for you," said the guard, as they headed to the elevators.

They agreed to meet in an hour. On their way down in the elevator, Matt told Joan about his previous meeting with Rutherford. When the elevator doors opened, they moved across the hall into Rutherford's office.

Molly Logan looked up. "Dr. Brenner, good to see you again. This must be Dr. Wu." She stood with her hand out.

"I'm Joan Brenner now." She reached for Molly's hand.

"Congratulations," said Molly with a pleasant smile. "Dr. Rutherford will be most happy to see you both." She released Joan's grasp. "I'll tell him you're here."

Molly returned and ushered them into Rutherford's office.

"Glad you agreed to see me. Have a seat," he said.

They sat in the two seats facing him.

"Have either of you accepted positions?"

"Not yet," said Matt.

"I've resigned my commission," said Joan. "We've decided to look for civilian jobs."

"Good," said Rutherford.

"We're still on our honeymoon," said Matt.

His eyes widened. "Congratulations."

Joan looked at Matt and then said, "Thank you."

"The security guard called me. He's found your things. So you saw the renovation that is in progress on six?"

"Impressive," said Matt.

"Much of the same thing is happening on five."

"I'm pleased the Army is gone, sir," said Matt.

"Thanks to you, Dr. Brenner."

Matt knew that he was only the catalyst and that the credit went to Rutherford.

The CEO looked at two folders on his desk.

"I have reviewed both of your personnel files. Impressive. Very impressive."

He turned to Joan. "We're building a new Alzheimer Research Center on five. I would like to offer you the directorship, Dr. Joan Brenner. Your mission would be to research the brain and study neurological diseases. Your expertise in pathology and cell biology makes you the best person for the job."

Joan looked at Matt. Her eyes told him she wanted it. He winked at her.

"I would be honored," she said.

"Now," he said, turning to Matt. "I know from our talks at Stanford, you had an interest in children's diseases. I'm offering you the director's position of our new Children's Research Center on six."

Matt sighed. For years he and Jack had talked about researching children's diseases, but he had forgotten he had told Rutherford.

"What do you say?" asked Rutherford.

"I've dreamed about working for you, sir."

Rutherford smiled. "Does that mean you accept?"

"One thing, sir. Would I be allowed to recommend an associate director?"

"You have someone in mind?"

"Peter Crane."

Matt crossed one leg over the other and waited.

"I know Dr. Crane's work. He would be excellent."

"Then I accept."

CHAPTER SIXTY-SIX

The next afternoon, sitting in the living room of their townhouse, the newlyweds celebrated their new positions at DnaTech with a glass of wine.

"Isn't life good?" said Joan, raising her glass.

"Now it is," said Matt, smiling.

The doorbell rang. Matt set his wineglass on the coffee table, rose, went to the door, and opened it. Dr. Keyes entered, tethered to Chris Cousins.

For a few seconds, Matt stood motionless, stunned by what he saw. Every muscle fiber in his body was as taut as piano wire.

Why is Keyes handcuffed to Chris' wrist?

"Hello, Fabor. What a surprise. Come in."

Matt led the way to the living room. Joan rose when she saw them enter. Chris moved Keyes ahead of Matt, went to the couch, and stood without saying a word.

"This is my wife, Joan," said Matt. "Joan, this is Dr. Fabor Keyes."

She smiled and then reached for his free hand.

"I've heard so much about you. Matt's talked very highly of you, Dr. Keyes." She turned and looked at Matt with a frown. Her body language asked him what was going on.

"Matt was the best scientist I ever had," said Keyes.

Everyone fell into silence. Matt couldn't keep his gaze off the handcuffs. No one mentioned them, and Matt feared his suspicion would come true if he asked.

Chris broke the silence. "You're talking to Mors."

Joan gasped, and a hand went to her mouth. Matt felt his world collapsing around him. He wanted to run out of the room and hide from the truth.

"There's some mistake," said Matt. "Chris, you must have the wrong man."

"He's definitely Mors," said Chris.

Keyes nodded. "I am he."

"Why… Why—for God's sake?" cried Matt, shaking his head.

"You'd never understand," said Keyes. "You're in a class with those who believe in Santa Claus and the Easter Bunny. You have too much faith in mankind."

"But we've won," said Matt. "Our system works."

"You haven't won. There will be others."

"Why?" asked Matt. "Why APAT?"

"General Taylor and I… well… we were fed up with the government. I tried to get the President to spend more money on antiterrorism, but he thought it was too costly. Congress sat on the money and Taylor tried to get to the Joint Chiefs to pressure the President and Congress, but the Chiefs thought they knew it all." He shook his head. "They're arrogant puppets of the Secretary of Defense, and the Secretary was in the pocket of the President."

Matt turned away from Keyes and saw the redness in Joan's eyes. Turning back to him, Matt said, "You were the President's Scientific Advisor. You had great influence in the scientific community. You could have used that influence to change the country. So many people respected you."

"You still don't get it," said Keyes. "You're like the politicians. There was no time to wait on the President or Congress with hundreds of terrorists filing into this country. Homeland Security was nonexistent. Something had to be done to protect Americans at home."

Matt sighed.

"You know," said Keyes, looking away for a few seconds, apparently in deep thought, "I once had planned to recruit you, but Taylor hated you."

Matt looked into his old mentor's intense eyes.

"You never would have recruited me, Fabor. I'd never do anything to harm this country."

"The world has changed," said Keyes. "We have a different kind of enemy like no other time in our history."

"Terrorists are fanatics, and many are uneducated and easily led," said Matt. "But you…" He shook his head. "God gave you a brilliant mind and look how you used it."

"Matt, you are not living in the real world," said Keyes. "We were prepared to save this country from the bureaucrats and the terrorists."

"That's insane," said Matt. "Omega Bytes would have killed

millions. And you know it."

"When APAT was captured by the FBI, and I learned we had only a few doses of antidote, I told Taylor to stop and let the FBI handle the terrorists. But he wouldn't listen. He went crazy."

Chris pulled on the handcuff and gestured for Keyes to stand. As Keyes stood, he turned and said, "I'm sorry I've disappointed you, Matt. Maybe someday you will forgive me." Then he followed Chris out the door.

Matt moved to the side-arm chair and flopped in it. He laid his head back and closed his eyes. After several deep breaths, thoughts of his father, Taylor and Keyes swirled in his mind. He saw each one for what they were. He wanted to hate them. Keyes, his surrogate father, for betraying his faith in him. His biological father for his stubbornness and for not showing him the kind of love Jack's father had shown Jack. And General Taylor for killing his best friend. But he couldn't hate them.

Fifteen minutes later, Matt called out to Joan. "I've something to tell you. It's quite important."

Carrying two cups of tea from the kitchen, she said, "I thought you might need some tea to relax you after that." She set a cup in front of him. "What is it?"

"It's about my father," he said, sitting up straight, and reaching for his tea. He took a sip.

Joan took her tea and sat in the other chair. "I wondered why you had never talked about your parents. What about your father?"

"We've had our differences..." he said, voice trailing off. "My mother was loving, but my father, well, he was cold and stubborn. We argued a lot. I guess it's partly my fault, but he got under my skin." He paused for a second, for what he wanted to say next pained him.

"My father didn't want me to go to college. 'Work the farm,'" he said. "'It'll be yours some day.' I've always loved science, but he never tried to understand me. We never talked again after I left for college." Matt took a sip of tea.

"I wanted my father to be proud of me like Jack's father was of him. Mr. Sinclair always encouraged Jack in everything he did. I craved that kind of attention, but never got it."

"You and Jack were really close, weren't you?"

"Like twins."

"I envy that kind of relationship."

Matt sighed.

"Matt, I'm sure your father is proud of you."

Matt looked into her brown eyes. "I was thinking. With all his faults and with only an eighth-grade education, my father is a better man than Taylor or Keyes, who I once thought were giants." He paused. "Unlike them, Dad would never hurt this country. He showed compassion to others. There were times I wondered why he didn't show his love for me."

"Maybe he thought you knew he loved you, or maybe he had a hard time showing his feelings. Did you ever think of that?"

Matt finished his tea.

"Sometimes we find it easier to show our feelings for outsiders," said Joan. "Maybe because we don't have to worry about making mistakes with them. Just like Kenny. He has a hard time showing his love for me. I think he's afraid of hurting me, but he does despite himself."

"You freed me of my burden when you came into my life, Joan. I've learned what love really is."

She squeezed his hand. "You must call your father, Matt."

"I will." He paused for one last thought. "You know something? Forgiving others really does work. It changes you."

"My, you've really gotten into a spiritual mood, Matt."

He smiled. "I believe I'll sleep better now."

THE END

A NOTE TO READERS

This is all fiction. The characters mentioned are not real. There is no DnaTech Pharmaceutical company in Clayton or in St. Louis, nor is there any secret Army facility there.

I make no claim as an expert in the biosafety labs. My research led me to USAMRIID, the CDC, and Richard Preston's books. I'm sure these folks will recognize certain liberties I took.

Thank you for reading my novel. I hope you've enjoyed reading it as much as I did writing it. If you liked *The Watchman*, I hope you'll look forward to reading *72 Hours* and my latest novel, *You'll Never See Me Again: A Crime to Remember*.

As an author, I greatly appreciate any and all reviews on my books, so if you can take the time to leave one where you purchased the book, I'd be grateful. Reviews help other readers find new books, and they're especially important to newer authors like me. Thank you for sharing your love of reading with others!

Every quarter I hold a drawing for a free, autographed copy of one of my novels. Please go to my website (www.robertamagarian.com) and sign up. In addition, you will receive quarterly newsletters and hear about any new releases.

Website: www.robertamagarian.com

Facebook: www.facebook.com/authorRAM

Twitter: www.twitter.com/authorRAM

LinkedIn: www.linkedin.com/in/robertmagarian

Email: author@robertmagarian.com

Goodreads:
www.goodreads.com/author/show/4019298.Robert_Magarian

ACKNOWLEDGMENTS

Thanks to my dear wife, Charmaine, who never doubted me, and our wonderful children, Bob, Paula, Cindy and Leslie, who wondered if Dad was ever going to give birth to this baby.

Special thanks and love to my granddaughter, Natalie Freude, who pushed me to put my thoughts on paper... "Why don't you just write, Grandpa?"

Many thanks to my writing mentor and friend, Robert Ferrier, for his direction, advice and encouragement.

My appreciation goes out to Dr. Ed Magarian for our many sessions, for reading the manuscript and for his advice and encouragement.

To Nancy Hancock and Jim Miller for reading the manuscript and for their suggestions. Thanks a million.

Special thanks to Hollywood-actor Christopher Cousins for allowing me to use his name for the Special Agent of the FBI.

Thanks to Sarah Whistler, Robyn Conley and Carolyn Wall for their suggestions.

ABOUT THE AUTHOR

Robert Magarian is the author of three thriller novels: *The Watchman, 72 Hours,* and *You'll Never See Me Again: A Crime to Remember.* In addition to his fiction, Robert is the author of two nonfiction essays, *Follow Your Dream* and *A Journey into Faith.* He lives with his family in Norman, Oklahoma.

www.robertamagarian.com